LETTERS
—FROM—
BRAZIL
IV

A Time to Hope

MARK J. CURRAN

Order this book online at www.trafford.com
or email orders@trafford.com

Most Trafford titles are also available at major online book retailers.

Print information available on the last page.

ISBN: 978-1-6987-1027-3 (sc)
ISBN: 978-1-6987-1028-0 (e)

Trafford rev. 11/15/2021

www.trafford.com
North America & international
toll-free: 844-688-6899 (USA & Canada)
fax: 812 355 4082

EPIGRAPH

"This Too Shall Pass."

PROLOGUE

The vagaries and vicissitudes of life, or its joys, challenges, and new adventures, your truly has experienced it all the last thirteen years. It is now 1984. Nossa! So much water under the bridge that it is getting hard to remember! What I thought would be a relatively short hiatus from my academic love of Brazil and my own real – life romantic love turned into what shall we call it, not a detour but "under construction" - a couple more lanes on the freeway that had to be built. Belaboring my weak metaphor (the reader knows I am good at reporting on history, literature, and even poetry, but not writing the latter), there were "construction ahead" signs, a few warning signs like "slow down" or "resume speed," or just "keep going, you are almost there!" Ha! For that handful of readers who remember "Letters from Brazil" or even "Letters from Brazil II and III" there is a lot of blank space to fill in since 1971. I'll try not to be a windy professor, that is, in continuing with the matter of filling in at least part of those blanks.

My time in research and why not say it, romance, ended abruptly in Brazil in 1971 when I was escorted to the Varig check – in line at the Galeão International Airport in Rio de Janeiro by a Brazilian security agent, but strangely enough, now good friend Heitor Dias. He of the Brazilian security police, the DOPS as everyone in Brazil mentions it, usually in a low voice – "Departamento de Orden Pública e Social" [Department of Public and Social Order], Brazil's big – time "cops." I had been asked to get on the Varig plane, the first flight out to New York City, with the words ringing in my ears, "You are not being ejected or thrown out of Brazil, just are simply being invited to leave," this by no less than General Goeldi of the Brazilian Censorship Board. Why?

Over a time of two years in 1970 and 1971 I had established a friendship and then a certain academic and musical partnership with one of Brazil's most talented and popular song writers and performers, Chico Buarque de Hollanda. Chico had once been dubbed the "unanimous favorite" of the national music scene for his work since 1965 and his blockbuster "A Banda" then and now an anthem for carnival in Rio. His intellectual pedigree cannot be improved upon in Brazil, his father Sérgio one of its most important historians, his uncle the same in linguistics and the man behind Brazil's most popular and academically recognized Portuguese Language Dictionary which became known by its nickname – O Aurelião – the augmentative form of the uncle's first name and a big joke: Aurélio's Big Dictionary. Chico started out as a teenager composing simple lyrics largely based on carnival and samba. But ironically with the dictatorship and its censorship he evolved through no choice of his own into perhaps Brazil's most sophisticated composer who invented all kinds of verbal tricks to "driblar" [a soccer term used when one player outmaneuvers another] the censorship board. And he got into trouble, lived one year in exile with wife Marieta in Italy, returned with Marieta and now a baby, and suffered the vicissitudes of dodging the critics in order to simply survive at his trade – the composing, recording and performing of popular music in Brazil. All that aside, he is good, and his music is good, a national treasure.

My link, hero worship on my part, was to a tiny segment of his dozens of songs, to the samba "Pedro Pedreiro" ["Pete the Laborer"] which tells of the life, dreams, and indefinite future of a poor migrant from Brazil's Northeast trying to scratch out a living in São Paulo, but always wanting to return – when things get better – to his beloved homeland in the dry northeast. It is coincidentally very similar in theme to what has been called the "Northeastern Anthem" by the great forró singer Luíz Gonzaga – "Asa Branca" – [White Wing]. However, and this is my connection, it utilizes the same theme as dozens if not a few hundred of the story - poems of the "Literatura de Cordel" [popular literature in verse] my study specialty in Brazil.

To cut to the quick – having all this as a dream, I was introduced to Chico by a girlfriend who knew him in school, we clicked with similar interests and via interviews and articles publicizing Chico's song and the northeastern folk – popular poetry link. The surprise was a memory trip to our growing up in the 1950s and a mutual love for old U.S. Rock n' Roll. After a quantity of beer and cachaça one afternoon at his house, both of us playing guitar and singing the old tunes, he proposed an L.P. as a joke, but he surmised to become a sure best – seller in Brazil. I sat in, he and his group did the heavy work, and it became a minor success in Brazil. The people were so starved for anything from Chico, and enough of the "velha guarda" [old guard] and Chico's generation had fond remembrances of their own fling with rock n' roll in the late 1950s to make sales boom. The military censorship board could hardly complain about rock n' roll in English and the fact the "leftist" Chico was performing with a U.S. citizen! They allowed a short series of successful concerts in Rio and one at the Itaipu dam site – all to raise funds and publicize a campaign for jobs for the workers, until the stuff hit the fan in 1971. Vlado Merzog a major journalist in São Paulo and a principal reporter of São Paulo's TV Cultura (like PBS in the U.S.A.) was "called to testify" to defend his recent anti- government writings, and after a long torture session died in the building the military and DOPS used for such matters.

Chico abruptly cancelled the concert tour, his own private protest, and most of Brazil reacted angrily to this first of many later to be told episodes of military oppression, cruelty, torture and even death. Chico refused to compose, sing, or have anything to do with them. Therefore, we both appeared before General Goeldi of the censorship board who asked Chico to resume the concerts as a "good will gesture." Chico refused and I was in the room. That was when I was asked to get on that Varig jet to New York. I told all this in "Letters II and III" published in New York City with the backing of friend and part time employer James Hansen of the International Section of "The Times." I sub – titled "Letters III" with the words "Good Times to Bad Times" and figured then to be absent from Brazil for an indefinite period of time into the future, as long as the dictatorship held sway. That happened, mostly. The low point was news from Chico about one year later when he and Milton Nascimento, another star singer, wrote and performed "Cálice." It means "chalice" in English, but in Portuguese it can have an altogether different reading when one realizes it is a homophone, a word spelled differently, sounding the same, but with a different meaning. Everyone caught the play on words, that it was "Cale-se" in Portuguese. That means in a nice way, "Be silent," and that is what happened to Chico, his colleagues, the press, and TV for the next few years at the height of the dictatorship (or "dictatorshit" as someone in the U.S. called it).

A fortuitous turn of events followed. Falling from the "céu" or sky was a wonderful opportunity for me as a full – time assistant professor at the University of Nebraska in Lincoln (called the great American "sertão" or outback by half – serious Brazilian friends). Because of my book "Adventures of a 'Gringo' Researcher in Brazil in the 1960s, In Search of 'Cordel,'" I was invited in 1971 to be a lecturer on International Travel's expedition ship the "International Adventurer" for a thirty – day plus trip from Manaus on the Amazon to the tip of southern Brazil at Rio Grande do Sul. The DOPS allowed this participation because of practical concerns – it meant \$\$ for Brazil with a wealthy adventure ship and passengers stopping at most of the major ports – but also because I was doing cultural speaking, introducing Brazil to its "adventurers" as the passengers are called and <u>not</u> doing any research.

That trip in 1971 brought an unexpected but delightful reunion with Chico. He, his wife Marieta and his band were allowed on board for an evening and a concert (seen by those in charge as great public relations for a Brazilian artist of such renown to perform for a major United States travel group). It happened again in 1976 and a surprise reprise in 1977 in Lisbon.

I had been working my way through the academic ranks all those years and was an Associate Professor of Spanish and Portuguese through 1978. Between legitimate academic efforts producing several academic articles in respected journals and three respected books in Brazil, and now five travel – cultural books and three initial works of fiction based on Brazil, I made the decision to test the water in a more ambitious place. An old mentor (and he was truly old by now) at Georgetown, the director of the dissertation back in 1968, had unbeknownst to me been keeping track of my doings. Father Ricci (no claimed relation to the famous Jesuit Italian missionary of 400 years earlier in China and Japan) of Ph.D. alma mater Georgetown had contacted me, saying with the old guard faculty gradually retiring but the nationally known International Studies and State Department – Foreign Service Departments still in full swing, the university needed some new blood. "We've always got the full phalanx (is that the proper word?) of adjunct faculty from up at the Capitol. Those folks are not only qualified and, ahem, do no harm in the placement of our graduates, but they also love the change of pace and let's face it, the prestige of adding Academia to their government posts. We have retired senators, representatives, all kinds of retired diplomats and even military hierarchy who are willing to do a seminar each year. But the regular 'stable' of qualified profs always needed to be replenished.

"And you know, our degrees tend to the pragmatic side (could it be any other way with the Jesuits?) – government service here and abroad but also social service for mankind. We are proud of having several graduates in the hierarchy of CARITAS and UNESCO. We are not necessarily looking for publishing scholars with the baggage of very complicated critical theory. All those adjunct retired politicians write books and can do that. That's where you come in, Mike. You have a nice balance between the academic and pragmatic, so we would like you to return to Georgetown as an Associate Professor with tenure (a very special attribute to you) in our Latin American Studies Sector."

It was time so I did it, making the move back to Washington, D.C. in the Fall of 1978. The University of Nebraska had served me well, and I served it well in return. My boss at the U. of N. Language and Literature Department Dr. Halderson expressed regret but said such academic moves are common, "part of the game," and said he was not surprised in my case. And finally, he wished me well and guaranteed a final sterling letter of evaluation to be forwarded to Father Ricci. I would miss the closeness to my family in farm country in Nebraska, but the telephone and a flight from D.C. to Omaha made things doable. It was a whole new world that Fall, night and day in most every respect from university life in Lincoln, and D.C. brings me to the other very big chapter in life the reader needs to know.

Molly. This goes way back to graduate school days in 1966. With all those ups and downs since 1971 with my, ahem, escapades with Brazilian women and then an engagement, wedding date and plans set in motion, and then abruptly cancelled, Molly and I had been on a roller coaster. And then there was the complication with Amy, first fellow staff on "International Adventurer," then sometime lover, and my proposal back in 1976 which she turned down, or rather, postponed, and finally ended it all in 1977 after our expedition to Portugal and Spain. It was a mutual decision; we both said we were enriched by the experience, saddened to see it end, but both agreeing it was for the best. That was when I got back in touch seriously with Molly still working in D.C. We had always communicated occasionally but never with any changes in our now distant relationship.

Molly had not been exactly lonely during those years, and in fact drew close to her Jewish boyfriend from college days in D.C. at George Washington University. Sherman, yeah, that was his name. I never met him, but I heard a lot about him. They ultimately broke up; I'm thinking because of the Catholic (Molly) and Jewish (Sherman) business. Molly later would never talk about him other than saying he was an important part of her life for several years. Okay.

So, we basically started over again back in Washington, D.C. in the fall of 1978, taking it easy and very carefully. I was now 37 and she was 35. She had done extremely well in her full-time job at a medical book publishing company, final proofreading and editing, and I think her boss there, Jewish as well, liked having her around and consulting each day. With her previous study and interest in art, particularly Modern Art, twentieth century stuff, she was a part – time docent at the Corcoran Gallery and has connections to the entire art scene in D.C. This is not a small deal; Molly had received offers to do similar work at the National Gallery and so far, turned them down.

We had been gradually ironing out the wrinkles from separate past lives, including my amorous escapades but serious times with Amy from "International Adventurer" days. And no less serious times with Molly and Sherman. It was later that fall when we had "the conversation." And we came to the same conclusion: we had always been compatible, great friends, and good candidates to spend life together. I was sure my "wild oats" days were over, and Molly concluded as well that her intense individualism and sense of purpose in life had taken her safely to this time and place. Religion still mattered; we were both Catholic and although not the Catholics of our parents' days, the tradition was important. Our studies and now our jobs were all indicating a rosy future. I know it is a cliché, but among other important topics, she said her "clock was ticking" and she had always dreamed of having children and being a mother. On Christmas Eve of 1978 I proposed to Molly – for the second time. That beautiful lady said yes.

This time it all worked out, no complications, no changes of mind, no surprises. Well, maybe one complication. Molly insisted, and I agreed, we would be married in Washington, D.C. and not her hometown back in Oklahoma. There was another dynamic in this: her mother had been an important part of the wedding preparations back in 1970, and I could understand the emotional and financial strain of "déjà vu all over again." And now her daughter eight years later and older! The solution was a beautiful but small ceremony in the Dahlgren Chapel in June of 1979. My immediate family, Mom and Dad, sister and brothers and Molly's parents, brother and his wife were there. Best buddy from high school and his wife, and our mutual close friends from old Georgetown days were there as well. The best graduate school friend, genius, mentor and drinking buddy Don Mize was best man, the only time in his life he wore a suit and I had to help him tie the necktie. But he did clean up well and put the rakish French beret which he constantly wore into a suit jacket. His toast by the way at the reception came in three languages. We had decided to forego the traditional bachelor parties but had all of us in one of the party rooms down at the Dubliner. It got beery especially when brother Paul began singing all the old Irish ditties. And Don sang an off key "Folsom Prison Blues."

The ceremony itself was small and beautiful, in the Dalhgren chapel with Father Ricci officiating. Reception followed in Dalhgren Hall and then we were off on a short honeymoon to the Maya Riviera in Mexico. I'm sparing the reader all the details, but it went well. So, you say, what next? It took a while, but Molly became pregnant two years later, had a wonderful pregnancy and our first child Claire, a beautiful young lady, was born in the fall of 1981. We had really settled into marriage, and all was going well. Molly decided to be a "stay at home Mom" at least until Claire reached school age. The Medical Book Company people said they would wait.

1

BRAZIL BACK ON THE BURNER

Spring of 1984 marked a wellspring for me, settled in and working hard at Georgetown and finally a return to work and research in Brazil. Oh, I neglected to mention, aside from the "International Explorer" trips in 1973 and 1976, I was allowed a special tourist visa for one week in August 1981, to be a guest at the "50 Years of Literature" Celebration of Jorge Amado in Bahia, and a small monograph even came out during the festivities. But back to the matter of Brazil. Life is complicated, and Brazilian politics make life look simple! I'll try to *briefly* explain the events that led to my return to Brazil in June of 1984 and their relation to research on the "newspaper of the masses" – the "Literatura de Cordel," an odyssey interrupted in 1971. The numbers may make it clearer.

1. The height of oppression and censorship took place in the 1970s, Chico's song "Cálice" the last I wrote of in 1971. The Vlado Merzog affair had happened shortly before that; then came "silence."

2. The winds of change, or rather a slight breeze, came in 1974 when General Geisel of Rio Grande do Sul came into power, succeeding the hard – line President General Garrastazu – Médici. The MDB - "Movimento Democrático Brasileiro" [Brazilian Democratic Movement] token opposition party actually won a few seats in indirect state elections at the same time. But the Vlado Merzog affair (reported in "Letters III") had done a lot of damage to the regime, and Geisel in fact replaced the general heading the Second Army in São Paulo to try to mitigate detrimental public opinion.

3. December 31, 1978, it was four years later, and the end of the Geisel regime became an inflection point. The infamous IA – 5 [Institutional Act – 5] which instituted the dictatorship back during the days of the Costa e Silva regime in 1966 was revoked soon after, opening the flood gate more than a crack, bringing the return of all the political exiles to Brazil just a year later in 1979 and the beginning of the "political pot beginning to boil," paraphrasing the famous lines of cordelian poet Leandro Gomes de Barros writing of politics in the teens of the 1900s.

4. Indirectly it was a Geisel action of one year earlier that really mattered: he blocked the "election" of another hard -liner General Sílvio Frota to become the next "elected president" by the military. Instead, General João Figueiredo, a cavalry general and long serving servant of the regime was selected and came to power (although he would say later, he never wanted it and was not suited to it, more on this soon). President Figueiredo would see the return of the political exiles including the long ago communists of the 1940s through the 1960s, gone since 1964, now the true political "opening" of Brazil, the end of the two – party system set up by the Generals (ARENA and MDB since AI – 5), one final major act of terrorism – the bombing of the sparkling Rio – Centro Shopping Center early his regime in 1981, and the incredible national campaign for "Direct Elections Now" in 1983 and 1984. The resulting euphoria was really what brought me back to Brazil now in 1984 – the cry for a return to democracy absent since 1964: politics, carnival, and dancing in the streets.

With censorship and pre – censorship a thing of the past, my research interest - the "newspaper of the poor" by the "representatives of the poor" the "Literatura de Cordel" - was resurrected as well and reported on and even played a small role in the political times. This was my academic purpose in returning to Brazil. It became much more.

2

DÉJA VU ALL OVER AGAIN

Father Ricci and James Hansen of the "New York Times" were old buddies, a mutually beneficial relationship. Georgetown sent highly qualified Area Studies graduates to the "Times" who became stringers all over the globe, and if they did good work and things panned out, they became permanent international correspondents. In return, James and his colleagues in the International Section provided a steady stream of almost "instant" information to the faculty at Georgetown as well as reliable speakers for seminars, round – tables and such. I guess you could use the cliché, one scratched the other's back. And the School of Diplomacy and Foreign Service shared in the arrangement, Georgetown's main link to the government's INR [Institute of International Research] and its divisions throughout the world. I was constantly discovering that the Foreign Service was far from the only option for such people, but as faculty I caught some of the drippings from the pie, or maybe crumbs from the cake.

A joint Georgetown – NYT research and travel grant enabled me to get back to Brazil in the summer of 1984, a bit of a variation of the earlier arrangement back at Nebraska so many years ago as told in the "Times" sponsored "Letters II and III." The goal was to provide up to date, accurate information on the political, social, and economic reality in Brazil's quickly changing national political scene. "Letters" to the "Times" would happen again; the visa would be through the State Department's INR – WHA (Institute of International Research – Western Hemisphere Analysis) so I would have semi – diplomatic status. And most important, I could catch up on "cordel" and its own role of reporting on recent events. In those days, telegrams were still used and a curious one arrived to me in the office late in April. Telegram lingo is quaint:

> *25 abril. Stop. 1984. Stop. O Governo Brasileiro aceita a volta do senhor Michael Gaherty ao Brasil no seu rol de repórter do cenário nacional e pesquisador da Georgetown. Stop. Disfrutamos sempre de relações cordiais com o INR – WHA. Stop. Porém, certas ações do senhor Gaherty em 1971 e o convite de se ausentar do Brasil no mesmo ano trazem necessariamente certas condições. Stop. O movimento deste senhor será vigilado com cuidado e em todo momento. Stop. Os melhores desejos de seu sucesso no Brasil. Stop. General Erivaldo Goeldi. Departamento de Censura Federal, governo Figueiredo. Stop.*

> 25th of April. Stop. 1984. Stop. The Government of Brazil accepts the return of Mr. Michael Gaherty to Brazil in his role as a reporter of the national scene and researcher from Georgetown. Stop. We always enjoy cordial relations with the INR – WHA. Stop. However, certain actions by Mr. Gahertly in 1971 and the invitation to absent himself from Brazil in that same year bring necessarily certain conditions. Stop. The movement of this gentleman will be watched with care at every moment. Stop. Our best desires for his success in Brazil. Stop. General Erivaldo Goeldi. Department of Federal Censorship, the Figueiredo Regime. Stop.

Okay. So, I have freedom of movement to do my work, but I don't. Hmm. Sounds familiar.

Uh, that freedom does not apply to the sticky wicket and perhaps mysterious sphere of, uh, women, woman friends, and, uh again, sex. And, oh yeah, there is the reality of marriage and being a father. In all honesty, these are different times in almost every sense. Other than Cristina Maria, the other women in Brazil were what you might call "spur of the moment" adventures, and in my defense, were confessed to Dom Eugênio at the Benedictine Monastery in Rio last time around. He was a very understanding and, uh, worldly sort; I think he lived a bit vicariously just hearing of my escapades. Hmm. Maybe all priests are like that, "Tell me more my son." He did not say, "Go and sin no more." No. He just said to not forget the sacraments and that they are indeed here anytime.

Now, as far as I know, and really with no news since 1971, Cristina Maria probably finished Law School and is probably married herself with kids. I don't know that for sure, but she was a serious interest last time we talked, just a few days after I had "comforted" her in 1970 from a nasty breakup with Otávio her first fiancé and a real bastard. The reader of "Letters III" of course knows all this, but hey maybe I've got one new reader. There was a time back in 1969 when I fantasized that Cristina Maria and I might actually get married and have a life at some university in the U.S. That idea was squelched by her, and we both ended up saying we could not spend the rest of our lives in the other's country. But shenanigans with her were a major cause in the "bust up" with Molly I already mentioned.

More apropos to the current moment are personal life and moral beliefs. It was one thing being a healthy bachelor in Brazil, quite another now being married and with a beautiful wife and daughter. My own Catholic morality has these priorities. Molly did not question or even refer to past times in Brazil, but only said, "Be careful, you have two girls now waiting for you to come home!" I assured her I would do that and would count the days until I could see them again.

Okay. Runway cleared for takeoff.

3

D.C. To Miami and On To Rio

It was June 15th, Monday, bags were packed, a general research plan in my head, and documents in order, including that diplomatic status; I kissed Molly and Claire goodbye and got in the taxi to Dulles. I admit that more "devil may care" journeys as a bachelor to Brazil did enter the mind, but not for long. A new day and adventure Professor Gaherty! Eight years since those different days as cultural speaker on the "International Adventurer" and that reality. There had been that reunion with Chico Buarque and Marieta on board for the one – night concert in 1973, but the dark days of the dictatorship had not disappeared afterwards, and any "normal" research activity was so long ago and fuzzy to remember.

The flight to Miami was relatively short (one large bag had been checked all the way through to Rio, but in the Dulles Airport). Miami International was a zoo, like always. A Tower of Babbel of languages, some Portuguese, some English, but mainly Spanish, I'm guessing either refugees from various hot spots south of the border or rich Latinos on a lark to enjoy Miami nightlife and the beaches (which they always complain about, saying not as nice as at home, but I add, maybe safer), staying in their condos purchased with "get away money" and taking the kids to Disneyland in Orlando. I've been through the drill so many times, checking in at the international terminal, passport and visa carefully checked and photographed by the United people, a lousy sandwich and a cold beer before boarding the "red eye" all - nighter of six hours to Rio. Service was now "airline plastic" in tourist class, a TV dinner but a glass of wine to liven up the taste and two scotches later before I fell into a semi-drowsy state until 7:00 a.m. as the jet began its descent into Galeão International Airport. It's Tuesday, 3a feira.

Nossa! Last time flying into Rio was a long, long time ago, thirteen years to be exact (two times by ship in 1973 and 1976). It was the beginning of "winter" in the southern hemisphere so the clouds and fog and I daresay, smog, that greeted us were no surprise. There was the usual panicky cattle – car exit from the plane; I've never figured out why Brazilians are never in a hurry except in this scenario. They all know the customs lines don't change, slow with the chain – smoking bureaucrats manning the document check - in booths. So I was in no hurry, still really groggy and waking up from the flight. The slightly bored and a bit irritable bureaucrat (for this early in the day, maybe it was the end of the night shift) studied my passport with visa as though it was the first he had ever seen in his life. I'm thinking he does not see many INR – WHA type visas, but he kept looking at the photo, then me now with more than a receding hairline, and finally did the magic rubber stamp, handed me the paper (does it ever change?) that said: "DO NOT LOSE THIS RECEIPT; YOU WILL NEED IT TO EXIT BRAZIL." I've written before of my constant fear over the years of such a circumstance, losing it I mean. I never did, but I think my DNA worry – wart personality (from Mom) played a role.

The surprise, pleasant to be sure, was when I collected by bag, put it in the cart and headed into the baggage area – another worry – if you got the red light, they dissected your baggage. A very familiar figure was standing there in an anachronism of Rio clothing, still the white linen suit inherited from the British heyday in Brazil and a sporty straw hat, fedora style. Heavier than I remember, but the huge smile on his face and the embrace that almost crushed me, it was Heitor Dias of the Brazilian DOPS, dangerous cop but now respected friend. In fact, I considered it a bit of an honor the Military would send him to greet me.

"Arretado! [My nickname, 'Cool Guy,' given to me my Chico Buarque]. Que prazer ver-te de novo! Estou aqui para te livrar desta esculhambação da alfândega. Pegue a mala e vamos bater um bom papo."

"Cool Guy! What a pleasure to see you again! I'm here to free you from the bullshit bother of Customs. Grab your bag and let's go have a good catch – up talk,"

"Oi Heitor! I see the DOPS is wasting no time keeping track of me, but great to see you. Topo! [I agree.] But don't get me drunk before I get to a hotel!"

Heitor said no problem, and I got a ride in the black DOPS car to a quiet restaurant just off the beach in Copacabana in Posto VI. The driver dropped us off and Heitor marked a pick – up in an hour and a half. We settled into a quiet table in the back of the restaurant, first ordered coffee and "pão doce" and the conversation began. Heitor had seen me on "International Adventurer" two times, both in 1973 and 1976 (with a special invitation to see what an expedition ship looked like and to enjoy C and C – chat and cocktails – and then a nice dinner), and he never forgot. But now it had been eight years!

"Miguel, I've seen the entry documents and visa and know you are now 43 years old, I'm just a handful more than that! Porra! O tempo voa! [Time flies.] I also know you are married to, let's see, that old flame Molly and you have a child! Parabens! It was long overdue for you to settle down. And, porra! [not translated, a not very nice Brazilian swearword] you are in Washington, D.C. at Georgetown and out of the backlands of Nebraska. I never did want to visit you there, but D.C. is another matter. More on that later. I (we) know a lot more, but I'd like to hear it straight from you. Velho amigo, you've made my day. Finish that cafezinho and let's get a "choppe." I'm not officially on – duty, so there's no hurry."

"Topo, mas só um! [Okay, but just one!] Porra! It's good to see you after so long. No one better to be on my tail or to keep me posted on all the stuff going on. Heitor, I honestly don't remember you talking much about family, just those time – off escapades at the corner bar or at Maria Aparecida's place. Fill me in."

"Arretado, I'm married as well, a sweet girl from my hometown, beautiful, and mainly, understanding (if you see what I mean). We've got three kids, all in primary or high school, and that's enough! Dorinha is an accountant, good thing 'cause I can't seem to keep track of loose change, so we can afford some child care now and again. And that also because I am making a truly decent salary now as a Captain in the DOPS!"

'Pera aí! ["Hold it there!] Capitão! Porra! Heitor that is amazing, and I am so damned happy for you. You deserve it my friend. I'm surprised they let you spend time on such a small matter as me."

"Arretado, *they* don't. I'm in charge of the entire south Rio district now, so you will see some of my subordinates following you around, but this is special, and I'm giving you my new mobile phone number (it's a new contraption we just started using) for any emergencies."

"Heitor, you must be totally apprised of the times. As you can imagine I'm well informed on Brazilian affairs but can have no real inside knowledge like you. Can you bring me up to date?"

"You first 'Arretado,' then I'll fill in the blanks."

"Heitor, in the big picture, we know your term 'abertura' or political opening or easing began to slowly come with General Geisel's administration in 1974 to 1979. We know he had to face the 'oil crisis' of 1974 and so did most of us in the world. The bad times that followed affected all our economies. We know he wanted the maximum of economic development for Brazil with a minimum of 'security.' So politics are inextricably mixed. On the bad side, in spite of his good intentions Brazilians still remembered the Vlado Merzog torture and murder (the last straw that broke the camel's back and sent me packing home). The big 'whammy' came in 1978, almost all too much to get your head around: Geisel thwarted the hard – right and got General João Figueiredo in and most of all ended AI – 5. A tremendous change of affairs – exiled citizens allowed to return, habeus corpus restored, full political rights restored, and the indirect election of Figueiredo. Porra! The 'anistia geral' ['complete amnesty'] for all the political dissidents came along with the end of AI – 5, and that pesky pre – censorship that got Chico and me in trouble. The state legislature elections and gubernatorial elections with MDB have had gains, but mainly the entire 'anistia completa' and 'eleições diretas já' ['direct elections now'] have upended Brazil once again. Does that cover it?"

"Miguel, you are extremely well informed, most of which is in the now 'free press' and acknowledged by all, but it's only part of the picture, and is not altogether accurate. I don't know if you or any foreigner is prepared to understand what we, my government, and the military, since 1964 have really aimed to accomplish for the good of Brazil. And if you are aware of the 'still present dangers' facing us here in our winter of 1984. I will be the first to admit that our protective measures of the Constitution have occasionally been extreme and perhaps not well thought out, the Merzog affair at the top of the list.

"I guess it truly comes down to this: do you, do the Brazilians believe there was a real threat of Communism in our country and in fact in the rest of Latin America in 1964? If you know your history and current events, from Cuba to Nicaragua, to Colombia, Venezuela, Bolivia, Chile, Argentina and Brazil, there can be no doubt. Fidel Castro and Ché Guevara had *specific* plans to spread their vile beliefs and system to all Latin America. We in Brazil, General Pinochet and colleagues in Chile and the Junta in Argentina have been the front line in preventing that. And, most importantly, we did. (I could see where this was heading but had the common sense to not 'push it' – Heitor was in charge.) We got Ché in 1967, the major threat, and Fidel is still around but not really a threat to us now. Mike, there *were* plans for an uprising with Governor Miguel Arraes and the "Peasant Leagues" in 1964, and they were squelched by us. There were some unavoidable casualties along the way, what does the military say? Collateral damage.

"The return of Arraes, Brizola and others, the freedom of speech to the leftists "cassados" in 1964 like Jânio Quadros (including your friend Jaime Ferreira and his ilk) and now the whole 'Diretas Já' campaign certainly have put us on high alert. We will turn over power only when it is completely safe. It's getting closer, but that's not yet. So, Miguel why are you here and exactly what do you intend to accomplish?

"Heitor, I'm back as a sort of reporter for the "New York Times" in liaison with the International Research Bureau and its branch the WHA in Western Hemisphere America. I'll be writing new "Letters" to the "Times" (the old as you know have been printed now in three books in New York) about what I see, what I experience and my take right now on Brazil. Nothing secret, nothing underhanded, just basic journalism. I am hoping that the end of IA – 5 and the 'Pre – Censorship' is indeed a reality. In regard to my own research, I'll be seeing what the 'cordel' has produced involving recent events, and I'll catch up with Chico Buarque."

"Yeah Miguel, we did not particularly like the end of 'Letters III' and the story of Merzog and then 'Cálice.' But that is water under the bridge, nossa, 13 years, mostly small potatoes now. We can talk more about that later. I'm more interested in what you intend to do about all your old girlfriends here in town. Once 'Arretado,' always 'Arretado,' hein?"

"Heitor, I've been thinking a lot about all that. You know I'm Catholic, maybe not always the best of the lot, but still a believer. Fidelity in marriage is, for the Church *and* for me, a must and, pardon me, 'screwing around' with it is what they still call a mortal sin. But Cristina Maria Ferreira and Jaime Ferreira and his family were close friends, and hey, even Maria Aparecida, Cláudia and Sônia were pretty good to me. I am thinking of what we call 'renewing social contacts,' ['trazendo tudo ao dia'] but no more. Heitor, I was 25 the first year in Brazil, 31 when I was invited to leave by General Goeldi, and I'm 43 now. All those ladies are 13 years older too, and things are for sure not the same. I'm really out of touch with them all."

"Miguel, I cannot say the same. You know we keep files and that goes for all the Ferreiras, and, ahem, I still have an obligation to be sure Maria Aparecida's place is on the up and up. We can swing by some day and see her. There is lots of news on that ample front (he laughed to see if I got his pun), mostly good. She would be the first to say she is no longer a 'broto' or a teenager. Ha ha. I personally don't think you can keep it in your pants."

"Nor will you know 'seu Capitão!' I'm renting a small apartment in Copacabana, in Posto 1 near Leme. It's near to where one of my best students has settled in since he decided to take my professorial advice and check out Brazil. I can do swimming at the beach, have a shorter commute to the Casa de Rui Barbosa for research, and get the bus at the end of Copacabana on Sunday morning up to the Feira at São Cristóvão. And maybe over to Chico's as well."

We ended that first great conversation there. Heitor promised he would be in touch and soon, and that we had a lot more to catch up on. Heitor's guy drove me to the apartment in Leme with a view of the beach and the fishermen's rock; I planned to spend a lot of time out there kibitzing with the retirees and maybe fishing some myself. The apartment was small, but neat and well – furnished, including that most important of all Carioca appliances – a telephone. It had a small color TV rarely turned on, but a nice desk and lamp for work off the dining room. The owner Rui by name was an enterprising young Brazilian capitalist who in fact had two other apartments in the same ten – story building, one like mine and one much larger on the top floor where he lived with his wife and two children. We would become good friends in the next two months; he had done an AFS year in Wyoming (they always send the Brazilians to frozen tundra!) and was always glad to speak English. After a couple of beers, we ended up reverting to Portuguese.

4

SETTLING IN

The first thing I had to do was call the Ferreiras, first to see how Jaime was doing but also the whereabouts and circumstances of "old friend Cristina Maria." Remember it is now, nossa! thirteen years since I last saw them. I called Jaime and Regina's number, and this faint but somewhat scratchy voice answered, "Residência Ferreira, quem chama?" I recognized Jaime's voice, identified myself, said I am back in Rio and just want to come for a visit and catch up on our lives.

Jaime took a while, then put 2 and 2 together and said, "O' É o Arretado! Ou é o 'velho arretado?' (He laughed at his own joke.) Certo. Certo. Muita coisa mudada aqui mas nunca esquecemos de você! Porque não vem pra' almoçar amanhã? Ligarei para Cristina Maria e veremos se pode chegar também. Vida nova para ela também, muitas novidades, e todas boas!"

"Oh, it's 'Cool Guy! Or should I say, *old* Cool Guy? For certain. Much has changed here but we never forgot you! Why don't you come for the noon meal tomorrow? I'll telephone Cristina Maria and see is she can come as well. There's a new life for her too, lots of new things, and all good."

"Ótimo! Chegarei as 12:30. Pode ser? Okei. Tchau."
["Great! I'll arrive at 12:30 p.m. Is that all right? Okay. Bye."]

When I rang the doorbell the next day at about that time, there seemed to be a "committee" of greeters, an aging Jaime, his wife Regina also moving along in years, and this lady, how can I say it? Cristina Maria now at about forty years old!

12

I'm sure there was a bit of shock all around, albeit not expressed, at least not then. Healthy "abraços" all around, including a hug from my old girlfriend, flame and sometime lover. All with big smiles and truly glad to see me, and vice versa. We gathered in the old living room and there were two handsome boys now in their late 20s, Cristina's brothers. Her "little" sister was married and living in Brasília. So almost everyone was there from back to the moments of 1965 when we watched the National Song Festival on TV and Chico won with "A Banda" and shared the prize with Gerardo Vandré for "Disparada." (You wonder why I write of it, but that was what flashed through my mind.)

It was a bit awkward to be sure, but Jaime pulled out the scotch "aperitivos" and most partook. Ah, where to begin? It was not unlike meeting Heitor Dias and having to recall thirteen years of absence from Brazil. I won't go into every detail, but still most of the long conversation that day was important, for all concerned. Cristina Maria and I had parted friends, no more, no less; thirteen years had not changed that, so everything was "cool," right? Probably.

I had my briefcase with me, and that included pictures of the wedding, Molly and me, family and friends, and of course of Claire our three-year-old. Cristina Maria was prepared as well, and I saw pictures of her and husband, Sebastião Latoya and three young children, two boys and a girl. More on that later. We oohed and aahed and I'll talk of the particulars more as they come up. The basic news was Cristina Maria and Sebastião married in 1973 after both had finished Law School at the UFRJ, both were lawyers in what I gathered was a very prosperous firm specializing in business expansion, hedge funds and corporate finance. The kids had come in 1975, 1977 and 1979 (sounds like good upper class family planning to me).

Jaime explained that he was fully retired (Regina said, "Well, mostly") and the boys were doing a fine job at the concrete company. He spends a lot of time just following all the news and developments in these exciting times but is in the office – library each night writing what he hopes will be one of the best and certainly most accurate accounts of the last twenty years, including his own political career. Dona Regina mainly takes care of him, makes sure he stays on a rather strict diet (the heart attack was in 1970), exercises and limits the scotch and occasional cigars. He joked, "I'm one of those 'velha guarda' ["old timers from the '60's guys] you see out walking the Copacabana 'calçada' each morning and then drinking way too much coffee in the bars with old cronies." There was so much to catch up on, and everyone remembered small and large details from now almost twenty years ago, so as they come up and I think of them I'll let the reader know.

I said I wanted to be apprised of all the recent goings-on and politics, but Jaime agreed that *that* indeed would be a long conversation, perhaps for later. First, they wanted to know how the farm boy from Nebraska was doing. The reader knows much of this, so you can skip ahead if you want, but it's important to know what I told the Ferreiras and vice – versa. I tried to weave together all that had happened personally and professionally. The move from Nebraska to Georgetown U. and International Studies (they all applauded that, revealing that they surmised and wondered when I was going to get out of the "sertão americano"), my duties at Georgetown, but mainly the academic good fortune with two books in Brazil and three books in the series of "Letters of Brazil" backed by James Hansen of the "New York Times."

What was totally new and a surprise for all was the job as cultural lecturer on the "International Adventurer" for International Travel and the five trips, including Brazil and Mexico twice and Portugal and Spain later. They were a bit offended I had not been in touch in 1971 and 1976 in Brazil but understood that ship and shore duties simply did not allow even minimum time on my own. I took a deep swallow of scotch, looked over at Cristina Maria and told of the involvement with Amy Carrier on and off for six years, how that had not worked out (I did not say it was she who really ended it), and then the chance to get back on track with Molly took place in 1978. Cristina clapped her hands and laughed saying, "Ótimo! That would have been how I would have scripted it!" We all laughed, and I got a bit red in the face.

And finally, I brought them up to date on this summer's (for me) project, job with "Letters" to the "Times" and the link to INR – WHA again (they knew of the first phase of that back in 1970). How the U.S. folks wanted the current inside story on current happenings in Brazil. I would add the "cordel" reporting since "abertura," and checking in with Chico and Marieta.

5

THE INSIDE "SCOOP" FROM THE FERREIRAS

The political climate that June was tense in all Brazil. In effect, the future of the "Diretas Já" ["Direct Elections Now"] massive national movement was in jeopardy. It is a long story and one I am obliged to tell, but there are a lot of threads. Where to begin? I think with that afternoon long conversation at the Ferreira's.

So then it was their turn, primarily Jaime's but with "editorial" comments by Cristina Maria and her brothers with an occasional remark by Regina. All this happened during a leisurely meal and over good Brazilian coffee afterwards. Here's the jist of it, much I would be looking into at the Casa de Rui Barbosa "cordel" collection later. They tried to just limit it from 1971, and I may have missed some items, but here's what Jaime reviewed, slowly, step by step (it was all 'jotted down' in his memory). Like a schoolboy in history class, he took me though it step by step, hitting just the highlights in about two hours between dinner and coffee after dinner.

1. 1970. Federal, State and municipal elections were mostly won by ARENA (the government party). The Vlado Merzog affair was 1971.
2. January,1974. General Geisel was elected president. The "oil shock" with horrible ramifications for the economy had been in 1973.

   (The whole ten years from 1968 to 1978 was known by Brazilians as the "Era do Chumbo" ["The Lead Era"] of torture, oppression, and death.

3. Geisel started some reforms and was the first one to use the term "Abertura" [Political "Opening"].
4. 1976. The MDB (opposition party) wins more seats in congress.
5. April 1977. Geisel dismisses the congress, makes gubernatorial elections indirect. He creates the electoral college for the next presidential election.
6. Geisel fires far right General Silvio Frota who was expecting to be the next president.
7. May of 1978. The new steelworker and labor leader Lula heads successful strikes in São Paulo.
8. Geisel ends the infamous AI – 5 in January 1979. Jaime piped up, "Great! Guess what? I can vote again. But for what?"
9. Geisel installs General Figueiredo as the new president in 1979. He is the former head of the SNI (National Information Service, the data bank for the generals during the dictatorship). In August of 1979, the "Anistia Geral" ["General Amnesty"] is declared by Figueiredo after long political debate and protests. The economy turns bad on him, rampant inflation.
10. The opposition wins more seats in the lower house.
11. The Rio Centro terrorism takes place in 1981 but by police radicals.
12. In a major move in 1981 – 1983 the government party ARENA is dissolved by Figuereido and the new PDS [Partido Democrático Social] takes its place. The old opposition MDB now becomes the PMDB.
13. In 1982 there are parliamentary elections and the PMDB wins almost 50 per cent of the Chamber of Deputies (235 out of 479) and 15 of 25 of the Senate, and the governorships of São Paulo, Rio de Janeiro and Minas Gerais. The political tide is turning, all a result of the evils of past years and the end of AI – 5 (recall it was put in by General Costa e Silva in late 1968, this after the attempted assassination attempt on him in July).
14. As "Abertura" takes hold, coincidentally the economy goes sour. Brazil is now the world's largest debtor nation.
15. The "Diretas Já" movement takes hold in all of 1983 and in 1984.
16. Jaime lists the huge political manifestations, parades, and protests. Of note, one singer, Fafá de Belém, participates in them all and sings "Hino Nacional" before each, records it and it becomes a national best seller. She is

a supporter of Lula the upcoming PT ("Partido dos Trabalhadores"). Many other artists including Chico Buarque de Holanda will join her.

a. The first manifestation ["passeata"] in Pernambuco on 3-31-1983
b. November 27, 1983, Paecambu in São Paulo
c. January 25, 1984. Praça da Sé, São Paulo, 300,000
d. February 16, 1984. First Candelária parade, Rio. 60,000
e. February 24, 1984. Belo Horizonte, 300,000
f. March 21, 1984, Rio, second Candelária parade, 200,000
g. April 10, 1984, Rio, final Candelária parade, 1,000,000
h. April 16, 1984, São Paulo, the Anhangabaú Valley Park parade: 1, 500,000

(I wondered how did he keep this all straight? Turns out Cristina Maria and her brothers could have remembered the same thing, all indelibly printed in Brazilians' memories.)

Porra! *This* was what I had missed in Brazil, although much appeared in certain news channels in the U.S. by the relatively few individuals interested in Brazil, but certainly not the national populace. Cristina's brothers Jorge and Wálter and she herself told of marching in all three Candelaria Parades, "It was like carnival, percussion beating on pans, singing of the National Anthem. A great moment of euphoria for all of us." Jaime said, "I could have marched and not been arrested, but hey, the ole' ticker dictated otherwise, but it was all televised nationally. Brazil let out a collective sigh of relief at being free to be in the streets like Carnival after so many years of fear and silence. But, Mike, as you know the 25th of April changed all that." Cristina Maria intervened, "And hey, Mike, Chico recorded 'As Tabelas' celebrating the parades."

"Nossa! I'll be calling him very soon and getting caught up."

Jaime said, "There is the one huge 'bummer' – The Dante de Oliveira Amendment which would have brought direct presidential elections failed to pass on April 25th. General Figueiredo after that huge 'comício' [manifestation] in São Paulo did an about face and tightened restrictions again – press censorship and arrests. Just two days before the actual vote on April 25th he placed all Brasília on military rule (the vote would be in congress on the 25th), live TV and radio were cut, and the generals put the heat on the congressmen. The result was the Amendment needing 320 to pass, received 298 voted in favor, 65 against but 112 pro – government deputies abstained (you can imagine the pressure exerted on them) leaving the Chamber without a quorum, so the amendment in effect died. The result: the next presidential election would still be through the electoral college, indirect. But the public balloon had burst, a giant fizzle, but the damage was done."

The afternoon was getting on, Jaime needed a nap, so we all promised to get together again in a few days to see how my research was going. Christina slipped a piece of paper in my hand on the way out with her private phone number and just nodded her head. Okay. More on that in a bit. First things first.

6

AN "INTERVIEW" IN CAPTAIN DIAS'S DIGS

I know the reader may be getting tired of this, but I swear it's all true, déjà vu not only again but over and over again. Since at least 1969. As I was walking back to Avenida Nossa Senhora da Copacabana to catch the bus to Leme and the apartment, a black government car pulled up, the window down, and a voice saying, "Miguel, precisamos bater um papo" ["Miguel, we need to have a talk"]. Who else? Heitor Dias. I knew the drill, so I hopped in the back seat; Heitor was on the other side, shook my hand, smiled, and said, "O' Arretado! Couldn't help yourself, huh? Let's go down to my 'office' and I'll get your news."

He instructed the driver to drive to one of the old government buildings out in Urca, near the Rio de Janeiro State Police Headquarters. We pulled into a driveway, and he motioned for me to get out, now in front of what I would call a "standard government" office building. Drab yellow, a bit in need of paint, but with lots of probably one hundred-year-old shade trees and not too far from the Sugar Loaf Cable Car Station. We walked up the steps and down a hallway into a newly remodeled and air-conditioned corner office.

"Heitor, this is a step or two up from the old place, huh? I notice a nice office desk and chair, a decent divan and two easy chairs."

"É, e um frigobar detras da mesa. Sente-se velho amigo. Quer uma Brahma? Está geladíssima."

["Yeah. And a Frigobar behind the desk. Sit down old friend. Do you want a Brahma? It's icy cold."]

19

"Pois é. Só tomamos café depois do jantar nos Ferreira. So what's up, Capitão?"

["Of course. We only had coffee after dinner at the Ferreiras. So what's up, Capitão?"]

"Nothing to get too excited about, at least I don't think so. Just an update on your friend Jaime Ferreira and family. Anything to say before a question or two?"

"Well, Heitor, it was almost like old days but maybe with 'Back to the Future.' Have you seen that new flick? The hero is magically transported back thirty years and then through some hassles and adventures back to the present. I think today was just almost twenty years to 1966. Those harum - scarum days were a long time ago. Maybe I can save you some breath: Jaime Ferreira is in his 70s, living carefully after that heart attack your people brought on him back in 1970 downtown at the DOPS 'office.' His wife Regina takes care of him. Ha. Cristina Maria is close to 40, married and with three kids and doing corporate law. Her two brothers run the concrete company (by the way I saw where Itaipu was just inaugurated, about time!) They all walked in the Candelaria Parades, were ecstatic over the possible Dante de Oliveira Amendment possibilities and hugely disappointed the thing never got off the ground. I gave my news and that' pretty much is it."

"Miguel, about what I expected. Jaime and that whole crowd are legal now, but I think like you say, 'inactive' at the moment. I'm sorry about the heart attack, but business is business, and his contracts with Czechoslovakia and Eastern Bloc countries and old crony 'lefties' from then needed our surveillance. We see him out on the 'calçada' now and again, and you're right, he is doing no harm. But he is in communication with the old buddies, and it warrants watching. They have lots of reasons to see us gone. What I really wanted to do is to finish our conversation from just a few days ago. Just kind of catch up. There are two or three matters of mutual concern. Maybe if we finish in an hour or two, we can drive by Maria Aparecida's place and have you do another chapter in all your 'catching up?'"

"I'm not sure Heitor what the 'other' matters could be. Why don't you clue me in?"

"Pois, one *is* Maria Aparecida. The other perhaps a small matter, that big encounter in 1981 you had with our most famous commie, you know who, Jorge Amado. Porra Miguel! You know better than I all that history."

"Merda, Heitor, you've got to get over that. Maybe if you let me give you the 'short' lecture of say 30 minutes, about two Brahma Choppes for you, I could enlighten you. I swear we've had this exact conversation before."

"I doubt that 'seu arretado.' But I will let you buy the beers, even if they come from my own stash. I will repeat what I once told you, 'Once a commie, always a commie.' You indeed were in Salvador back in 1981 for that big 'groveling, bowing down' ceremony; it's in the official records and hell, you even made the national news. You know we never have cleared you of all those leftist sympathies. How do you explain all that? I wonder why we are friends."

"Heitor, I am as much a patriot as you, but just in my own country. You have just pushed my buttons. And my damned Ph.D. was to train future scholars of the *dangers* of International Communism spreading in the third world. But I guess you know we believe in Democracy and free speech! It was a miracle Bahia even happened, and it involves so many aspects of Brazil I could do a book just alone on that. I still don't know who convinced Itamaraty (the Brazilian State Department) to grant me that special one – week tourist visa in 1981 to participate in the celebration, this with my history with General Goeldi and Chico Buarque and the "invite" to leave in 1971. I think it must have been because Amado has a huge readership in the United States, is revered as one of your best, most readable writers, and his movies are big box – office in the 'foreign films' cinemas. The fact a North American had a recent book on him printed just for the "50 Years Celebration" might have also swayed the decision. I'll give you the short version.

"I did a short monograph on Amado's use of the "cordel" in three of his novels in a stay-at-home sabbatical in the winter of 1975. The people doing the publicity for the "50 Years" accidentally saw the book title at the Casa de Rui Barbosa where the manuscript was gathering dust due to their perennial lack of funding, talked them into a co – edition with the Cultural Foundation of Bahia, and did a big book party on it during the celebration. It was all 'accidental' and so Brazilian. It turned out to be one of the most felicitous moments of my academic career up to that point, bigger than that big conference in Rio – Niteroi you know about in 1973.

"The highlights of that one week in Salvador were a long two hours visit with Jorge, Zélia, João Jorge and the kids at Amado's house in Amaralinha, interviews with major newspapers, local and national TV, and a half page in color in 'Isto É' - all because of Jorge. Then TV again for the autograph party in a spanking new bookstore, the best of Bahia in a new shopping mall, Itameti or something like that. I was in seventh heaven and still can't believe it happened. Sitting beside Zélia and Jorge in a dinner at Camaféu de Oxossi's Restaurant in the Mercado Modelo, across from Vargas Llosa and wife Patricia. It's all a dream now, but like I always say, 'They can't take that away from me;' it happened.

"Back to your complaint. Yes, Amado was an avowed Marxist in his younger years, a national congressman for the Communist party in 1947 until he was kicked out of Brazil, and then was an activist in the 'Internationale' working doing Marxist propaganda via translation work in Budapest in the early 1950s. No argument. But in the late 1950s, he learned the truth of Stalin and the Gulag and reneged on Communism and Russia and returned to Brazil to the strictly private life of a writer. *That* was when the big change or perhaps can I say 'literary epiphany' took place. He stopped writing 'social realism' or as some say, 'socialist realism,' from the books dating from the 1930s and 1940s, and began to write much lighter, more entertaining and much more readable novels like 'The Miracle Shop,' 'Gabriela Clove and Cinnamon' and then 'Dona Flor and Her Two Husbands.' They all were made into movies, the latter by the Barreto brothers, no one more linked to capitalism in Brazil than they with the expensive color films. And that's when he matured into what most believe is Brazil's best storyteller."

"Hey, your 30 minutes are about up, and my beer is gone. It really doesn't matter how you dress him up, those twenty – five years as a card - carrying party member, thoroughly Marxist and in our national congress can't be swept under the carpet. Once a commie, always a commie. We'll have to agree to disagree."

"Heitor, can I just say Jorge Amado was incredibly kind and gracious to me; I was a young whippersnapper, a nobody, and he treated me like a close friend. And that tiny book and event probably swung the vote in my promotion to Associate Professor at Nebraska. I've got a copy or two of the 'Isto É' article, I should plasticize it for posterity, and you can see it. The only bad thing of the whole week was that 'xinxin de galinha, vatapá, abará, acarajé' and other Bahian 'delicacies' that left me with the worst stomach upset ever in Brazil, and there have been many."

"Está bem. Você desembuchou! [It's okay, you got it off your chest or was it your stomach! Ha ha]. What do you say we drive over to Aparecida's place? Topa?"

"It's late in the afternoon, so I guess we are still ahead of 'rush hour' but it won't be a long visit. Topo."

7

SANTA MARIA APARECIDA AND THE MIRACLE

Heitor's driver picked us up and drove through the late afternoon traffic coming from Copacabana, moving through Urca and on to the Aterro, around the bend in Flamengo and pulled off in the middle of that long beach in front of the old historic palatial house which was "home" to the ladies. Readers of past "Letters" may recall the place. I certainly did. It's still funny to me that the star prostitute took her name from Brazil's most famous saint, Our Lady of the Appearance [Nossa Senhora da Aparecida], Brazil's equivalent of Fatima or Lourdes. But like Maria told me, it was just obeying the Catholic tradition of taking the name of the saint on the day you are born. Voilá! She may have reminded me of that when I was snuggled up against her voluptuous body in the "office" on the second floor of the palace. But just like the rest of the "cariocas," thirteen years have passed for Maria, so …

We were greeted like old friends at the door by Maria herself, rushing forward to give me a huge "abraço" and shouting, "O' Arretado, nunca esperei ver-te de novo!" [Oh, Cool Guy, I never expected to see you again!] She then hugged Heitor saying, "Você, velho cabra da peste! Faz tempo, bem vindo." ["And you, you ole' son of a bitch! It's been too long. Welcome back."]

We all sat down on a comfy divan in the "living room" and Maria remembering I liked a good scotch, called for one immediately and a caipirinha for Heitor. She was much the same, just a wee bit heavier, but not enough to take away from the splendid figure, and "dressed for business," revealing it all. Like any woman, she spied the wedding ring on third finger, left hand, smiled, and said, "That's no problem here, querido, we can all keep a secret. Let's go up to the 'office' and get reacquainted. I can always make time for my favorite 'gringo.'"

I went along with it all, but my mind whirring and wondering how I was going to remain faithful to the wedding promises and to Molly, determined intellectually before the trip, but this was different.

But Maria surprised me. After we went into her rooms, she pouring me another healthy scotch, she did plant a long kiss on my lips, enough to get the old stallion excited in the mares' corral, saying, "That was just saying 'Thanks for the memories,' like your famous Bob Hope says in his programs. Miguel, you always respected me, treated me like a lady, and I can certainly respect your new status now, even though it won't be easy. You are obviously at a different point in life."

"Maria, not easy for me either, but the right thing to do. Let's swap stories, and just friends, okay?"

She shrugged her shoulders and said, "You first."

I filled her in on all the reader already knows, work, Molly, marriage, daughter Claire, and now a return to research and work in Brazil. She said she really could not complain about all that, wanting the best for me, and dabbed a bit at her eyes while saying it. I asked, not sure if I was interfering with "work" time or not, to tell of her life all these years.

"Miguel, it's good and bad, but mostly good. You remember my education, but also that there was no way to make a living as a teacher even with a degree in literature from a good university, not without family connections in this Brazil. And porra! I like what I do and I'm good at it. You need business sense and some decent managerial talent to run a place like this. I can tell you, but not the girls, that I am more than financially set when the time comes to leave the 'castelo.' I've got a nice condo in Leblon on the beach where I am known as respectable Senhora Vieira, a business lady from São Paulo (true in a manner of speaking!) who visits Rio on the shuttle once a week. You know I know lots of men, and many of them the 'shakers and movers' in Rio, so if I want company, I can have it on nights off. What I think I'll really do, and maybe just in a few years, is travel, see the places I've studied about, and take along someone to keep me company. If you were available, you would be first choice!

"I did go to the Casa de Rui after you left and like I promised, went to the reading room and delved into your 'Literatura de Cordel' world. What an amazing journey you have had here in Brazil, all the way from the boarding house days in Recife, collecting 'cordel,' to meeting Chico Buarque and making your own life in

24

America." She laughed, "I would not have turned that down 'querido.' But there you have it."

"Maria Aparecida, it appears things have turned out well, as best they could. Do you want to tell me how it's been for you as a citizen and business lady, with the military, the regime and all the ups and downs since 1971, and now the 'Diretas Já' business?"

"Miguel, that is a very long story and I think you and I should have a respectable night out, dinner and drinks maybe at this elegant and intimate place near me in Leblon and I can tell you all about it. Suffice to say, many of our best customers have been closely involved in all that government business, and I was indeed apprised, shall we say, between 'takes.' How about a date, no funny business, and you shall get stories and angles of it all you won't get anywhere else. It's safe to talk these days, but still, we have to be careful. And, oh, by the way, Heitor could tell you some scary stories of these past few years. I'm sure you are smart enough to not make waves, huh?"

"Maria, this is terrific; I should be here for at least six weeks, so we can 'do' the dinner on your day (or is it night?) off. But can I use the information from you, edited of course, in my letters to the 'Times?'"

"Heavily edited my friend, but still interesting enough to keep your readers' attention. So, I have to go, people to see, if you know what I mean! Ha ha. Maybe Heitor has finished his 'business' by now, remember, he's all Brazilian and most Brazilian wives 'understand.'" She laughed, kissed me again, and escorted me downstairs. Heitor was indeed waiting and said, "Foi rápido Arretado! Você está fora de forma! Bora, obrigações, sabe." ["That was quick, Cool Guy! You must be out of shape. Hey, let's go, obligations you know."]

It had been a very long and eventful day in Rio, and what can I say? I felt back at home. But tired, very tired yet still from the flight and settling in. Heitor dropped me off at the apartment in Leme, I had a quick supper down at the beach and crashed. Tomorrow another day.

8

A FISHERMAN'S LIFE

The next morning, I met my former student from the Georgetown Portuguese classes, my most successful. Why? He was instilled with such a love of Brazil from the classes so that when he went to Rio in 1980, he never came home. A long story. ["História larga."] Flávio Pagano Friedrich was born in Italy, raised in Chicago and went to school at Georgetown because his parents wanted a Jesuit education for their gifted son. I passed on to Flávio and his good friends in Portuguese 101 a love for the Brazilian variant of Portuguese, but also of Brazilian music, food, beer drinking on Friday after class, and the memories of Carnival I brought home with me from stays in Brazil. Not the least was the showing of "Orféu Negro" or "Black Orpheus" in class each year at Carnival Time. Maybe that explains it: Flávio picked Leme, actually a small, modest apartment in back of Leme next to the main street leading up to a "favela," Chapéu Mangueira, as his "home" in Rio.

Actually, Chapéu Mangueira and Babilônia "favelas" are connected, the latter with the spectacular view over to Botafogo Bay, Urca and Pão de Açúcar, the former with a view of "A Pedra do Leme" and the Copacabana beach, waves, and mosaic "calçada." This particular morning, we swam in the waves of Posto 1 in Copacabana, strong enough to do some body surfing or "fazendo jacaré" ["making like an alligator"] as the Cariocas call it. It had been a long time, I was thirteen years older, and maybe not in the condition of last times in Rio. Whew! No accidents, "graças a Deus," but exhausted as we sat on the beach to rest. My god, Rio was beautiful, and it was all coming back to me.

After breakfast at a "boteco" or "pé sujo" along the beach, but still in beach attire of swimsuit, t-shirt and sandals, Flávio ceded to my wish to walk to the big rock at the end of the beach and along the narrow walkway where all the men and boys with time on their hands, a truly mixed crowd of Cariocas living in Leme and people from the "favela" including many retirees, were fishing. It was a bit scary at first. They are fairly high up off the water with long rods, large reels and casting far out into the waves crashing on the rocks below. I think it requires some period of learning how to do this and getting the "knack" for it. We watched for a while, chatted a bit with a few of the fishermen (Flávio knew one or two of them from the "favela"), and I begged off an invitation for some beer drinking, still with jet lag and needing rest. We had each other's phones, so we planned for a bit of "farra" ["partying"] the next weekend. Flávio was working way up in the north zone at a major publisher of textbooks for studying English, doing writing and editing, and also teaching free-lance English classes for some very upper-class Brazilians. "Inglês para executivos!" he said, and laughed. I had research to do, so we tabled it all for now. Adventures, however, were on the way.

9

Back To The Casa De Rui Barbosa

Friday, 6a feira. The next morning I took the downtown bus at that broad thoroughfare before the tunnel to Urca, Avenida Princesa Isabel, and got off at the stop on São Clemente in the middle of Botafogo and did the fifteen minute walk up to my old research hangout. Lots of feelings and thoughts can go through your mind on such a jaunt, all dating back 18 years to 1966 and my initial time there. A good one – paragraph review is in order.

The sophisticated Casa de Rui Barbosa in Rio, home, research center, library, and nature park on the original estate of said diplomat, intellectual, bibliophile, one of the founders of the Hague, and candidate for president in Brazil, had a funny quirk: by one of those "accidents" of Brazilian culture, it came to house in the early 1960s the best collection of Brazil's "literatura em verso" or "literatura de cordel." The "cordel" at that time was totally looked down upon by the intelligentsia of Rio and Brazil (other than a handful of folklorists) as an unsophisticated "poor man's literature." It was only an "accident" it was collected and housed at the Casa de Rui (to be shunted into a corner of a small mini – library annex next to the main house and library) – this by virtue of the Department of Philology as a "remnant of the popular speech of Brazil." It was there in 1967 I read a few hundred of the broadsides of the "cordel," taking handwritten notes on 3 x 5 index cards of most of the story-poems written by "cordel's" best writer, Leandro Gomes de Barros, and all became the basis for the Ph.D. dissertation.

Visits and research continued in 1969 and many years thereafter. Some of my best friends in Brazil worked there, people I shared the "blue plate" lunch with across the street for days on end and I sat across from in the research library, foremost among them Sebastião Nunes Batista. Now in 1984 many were deceased, retired, or had left Brazil for better academic jobs and greener pastures elsewhere. That morning I was re-introduced to an old friend and mentor, the writer Orígenes Lessa, major short story writer in Brazil and pioneer patron of the "cordel," especially in Bahia (with connections to Cuíca de Santo Amaro and Rodolfo Coelho Cavalcante). In addition, and not small potatoes, he was the owner of an excellent private collection, one of the best in all Brazil. Orígenes was now "chefe" or head of the "Cordel Research Library and Collection." We had an important but very brief initial meeting back in 1966 when I was informed he was an "essential source" for the dissertation research, and we kept in touch all those years, me reading his seminal studies on "cordel," he following my work and young career. We "clicked," on the same page intellectually and "philosophically" via a common sense, historical – journalistic approach to the "cordel."

"Miguel, que bom te ver! Faz tanto tempo." [Mike, how good to see you; it's been so long."]

"É, Orígenes, igual! Muito feliz a ve-lo." ["And you Orígenes, how happy to see you!"]

Orígenes called for "cafezinho" and soon we had those tiny demitasse cups of piping hot, sweet, black coffee poured from a thermos from the research center's kitchen. It was standard procedure at business and government offices and even libraries for the coffee ladies to make their rounds. A great custom! I cannot help but remember the good friend who suffered a heart attack and admitted later he drank more than 20 per day! But this is what keeps you going in Brazil! Orígenes was older (weren't we all), greyer, a bit stooped, but still with that sparkle in his eyes and as I would soon learn, the same devilish sense of humor.

"So what brings you to see us after so much time? We kept up with you and Chico on that turné [concert tour] in Rio, São Paulo and Itaipú in 1971. I knew Vlado Merzog when I was doing publicity for Esso in São Paulo way back in the 1950s. Nossa! It could have been me in that room. You were right to get the hell out of Brazil! But, hey, it looks like we are on to better times. The political pot is boiling, almost like back in the Kubitshek, Quadros era! I can only surmise you've come back to take up where you left off, reporting on "cordel," but frankly I think your sex life would be a helluva lot better on tour with Chico. All those funky groupies ["brotos"] fell in love with you! By the way, I've read all the 'Letters from Brazil' books, all three, so you don't have any secrets from me. Ah, to be young again. I'm still trying to decide which chick was my favorite. Oh, you may meet one of them back in the "cordel" check – out section. Discretion does not permit me to mention names."

"Orígenes, that was thirteen years ago! Things have changed a bit, but I will have to say hello if I see someone I used to know. Ha ha. But pardon me, I did not expect to see *you* here. In fact, Sebastião across the room is the only familiar face. What happened to Arnaldo and the other guys in the Research Section?"

"It's a long story Miguel, but here the short of it: Arnaldo suffered a heart attack two years ago and is retired at home with his wife Eneida. He still can write, does some private tutoring of those rich people trying to pass the Portuguese exam for Itamarati, but was unable to continue full time here in the Research Center. That's when Presidente Américo gave me a call. Miguel, there are not that many of us old farts around who even know what "cordel" is about, and I'm not getting any younger. You want a job? Ha ha."

"Naah! But they've got the right man for the job, other than Sebastião, you may know more about "cordel" than anyone. ("Except you," he said.) I'm here to fill in the blanks since AI – 5 and 1971 and I expect there's a lot to see."

"Yes, and no. The bottom really dropped out of production with the 'censura previa' but the floodgates opened in 1978 with the end of AI – 5 and the censorship. However, our most famous horse's ass, oops I'm sorry, Cavalry General, President Figueiredo is under all kinds of pressure to keep the heat and the lid on, now that Dante de Oliveira failed. Indirect elections are set for just a few months and there is a flood of behind the scenes infighting in congress and the military and on the left from the PMDB and Lula. Porra! I got off the subject.

"We have been continually supplied with anything new in 'cordel' that has come out, from Sebastião and his connections up at São Cristovão, from Franklin Maxado in São Paulo, and Joaquim Batista de Sena in Fortaleza."

It was at that point that Sebastião came up, gave me a huge "abraço," saying how much he and others had missed me, I, practically an unofficial fixture at the Casa research table and the "cordel" stacks. The feeling was mutual, and I guaranteed him we would go back to the "prato do dia" place for lunch and I'd get my chair across from his in the library. And maybe we could go to São Cristóvão together.

"Domingo que vem. Vamos!"

Over another "cafezinho," Orígenes explained that his one – half day commitment at the Casa still left him time for writing and homelife with Maria Eduarda, promising me dinner and talk the next week. "Miguel, other than what we've said, the 'cordel' side of things has been altogether too quiet. The Casa's budget was cut these last years, and as you know, the Rui Sector gets first choice on funds for publication. We've managed a small monograph or two, but that's it. There truly is not much middle or upper class interest right now; even Ivan Cavalcanti Proença with all his prestige could only bring a small crowd to an event a month ago. But the story – poems are out there for your purposes!"

The phone rang, it was the library, and they said the call was for me. I think I was a bit surprised and maybe a bit embarrassed; the voice was familiar. Cláudia of the old Rio – Niterói Conference days. She wondered if I could drop by and say hello after Origenes finished, "So p'ra matar saudades, mais nada." ["Just for nostalgia, no more."]

Orígenes had to go to a strategy meeting with the head of the Research Center, so we agreed I would call him and come for "almoço" sometime next week. And I agreed to meet Sebastião at his place in Glória Sunday a.m. and he would be my "cicerone" once again to the fair. Terrific. They both smiled as I headed over to the library, Sebastião saying "Não se esqueça do 'Pinto Pelado,'" ["Don't forget the 'Naked Chick',"] winking at me. I'll tell you sometime what that means.

I took the elevator from the Research Center down to the next floor which was entirely dedicated to the new library, a far cry from pre or should I say no – technology days in 1966. I recognized two or three faces of the ladies back from the big conference and then party in 1971, but then was ushered into Cláudia's private office; she was now head librarian for the "cordel" section, no small affair. She greeted me with a warm abraço, me feeling once again that voluptuous body and maybe involuntarily reacting a bit to it. Damn. It's like that greeting card with the doggy in the poker game with four aces, saying to itself, "Don't wag tail. Don't wag tail!" She smiled knowingly but said, "Arretado, don't get worried. Have a seat over here on the other side of my desk. It's been such a long time and so many changes, but I have nothing but wonderful memories of our 'break' from those boring old academic talks at the conference back in '71. You look almost the same, handsome as ever, but do I notice a bit higher forehead and maybe a larger belt size? Ha ha."

"Cláudia, you look terrific! 'O passar dos anos te tratou bem.' ["The passing of time has treated you well.'] And yes, 'as águas rolam,' lots of changes and mostly good."

"Miguel, I'll cut to the quick. I'm giving you my private phone number and please call me soon. I think a drink or two at a nice bar overlooking the beach would be a much better place to catch up. Who knows what that might lead to?"

"É, Cláudia, concordo e topo, mas tenho que dizer – te que os tempos mudam, agora sou homem casado, e com uma filha. Não pode ser o mesmo de tempos atrás."

["Yes, Claudia, I agree and it's a date, but I have to tell you that times have changed, I'm a married man now, and with a daughter. It can't be like it used to be."]

"That's not so different with me either, but we've got to have that drink. Will you call? If we have to, we can talk about the 'Cordel' Collection and all the innovations in the library. Make it mostly business, 'topa?' If you call Monday, we can do it after work about seven and you can buy me dinner. I think we will have a lot of fun and a nice reunion."

"No harm in that; I'll call Monday." That carioca "air kiss" and "abraço" followed, not as close as the first one. Sofia said, "I don't what you to be embarrassed walking out of the office. The girls will be watching. Tchão, querido."

10

"HOJE É SABADO!" (VINICIUS) DIA DE MÚSICA

Never a dull moment, after sleeping until 9:00 and just barely finishing the "café com leite" and "pão e manteiga," that carioca eye-opener (I haven't mentioned that Rui my landlord sent his own maid Marcela down each morning to provide such wake-up goodies), the doorbell rang, and it was Flávio once again. We had talked about doing something today, so it was no surprise. He was dressed for the beach, "sunga," carioca sleeveless "muscle" t – shirt, flipflops and towel, and a personal bit of the times: a U.S. style baseball cap worn with the bill facing the back. (The heroes of my youth Mickey Mantle or Yogi Berra would not have approved.) I changed into swim attire and off we went, a repeat of swimming, body – surfing and then an icy cold "choppe" at one of the beach bars. He wanted to know how I was doing, getting used to Rio again, and proposed a full day's activities.

Saturday, incidentally his big day off from work at the publishing house, was "feijoada" day in Rio's bars and "botequins," especially up on the "morro" in Chapéu Mangueira behind his apartment house, but when I said I could not handle that spicy black bean stew, he laughed, saying he should have remembered that from the lectures at Georgetown – the "gringo" with the world's most delicate stomach! "But we have to go up on the 'morro' and over to Babilônia to see the view. It's best after the morning haze has burned off, oh well, another day."

We had the old standby, "bife com arroz, vinaigrette, fritas e salada de legumes" at the same beach restaurant and two or three more choppes. Conversation was great with lots and lots of laughter, Flávio could have been a stand-up comedian

33

with ongoing ribald comments on the cariocas and tourists who walked by the café. We basically were still catching up on his days in Rio since 1980, all the ups and downs of his finding a job, including the "jeito" of arranging a work visa. It took a "despachante" and two bribes to get it done. I was drowsy after the meal and the beers and proposed we go home, shower and I would have a nap. After that Flávio had plans (he remembered to a fault all my stories from my own days in Rio in 1966 -1967 and 1969). We would go downtown via the new subway to the Rua da Carioca and the place I bought my Brazilian rosewood guitar in 1967: the Guitarra de Prata. That's what happened.

At about 2:00 p.m. we walked over to Princesa Isabel again, but this time got on the new subway to downtown. It was a very "un-Brazilian" experience, maybe because the line was new, just two months old. The escalator down to the tracks worked smoothy, and on its walls and that of the station itself there was not a speck of graffiti and no advertising other than the signs of the Rio de Janeiro Transportation network bragging about the construction in record time! Just the information electronic signs up above. In three minutes, we heard the train whistle, the announcement of the arrival on the P.A. (and in a clear Portuguese I could understand!) and whoosh, the car arrived, doors opened, and we walked into just a moderately full car. Flávio has two different theories on the cleanness: Cariocas want to "one – up" with their neatness the Paulistanos who have had metro service for years, or, they are in a state of shock and too timid to mess things up. He laughed, saying they will soon miss all the graffiti, the loudness of passengers, and the views of the beaches, tunnels, cars, pollution, and general "bagunça" ["mess" or more colloquial, "f******* mess"] of the bus lines.

It reminds of the joke of two Brazilians who arrived to the new, cold, severe, antiseptic, Galeão International Airport a year ago. One said, "Oh, I miss the old, crummy hot terminal, the crowds, the noise, the surly clerks at the airline counter, and the even more surly baggage guys." Another said, "You mean all that 'bagunça?' Are you crazy?" "Well, at least it's *our* "bagunça."

In twenty minutes, we were off at the Rua da Carioca station, up the escalator and out onto an incredibly busy street. It had been a long time, and lots had changed, but Flávio led the way and soon we were in front of a glassed in, modest storefront with "A Guitarra de Prata" stenciled on the glass. I have to admit, there was some emotion when we walked in and it seemed just like I remembered: very dark, wooden paneled, a main display case with perhaps five or six beautiful guitars on stands, and many tall, vertical wooden cupboards which we discovered held more guitars carefully placed in cases.

A young clerk – salesman approached us, wondering of our exact purpose, sensing "gringo - $$$ - filé mignon," but I asked if there still were any personnel from years earlier around, saying I had bought a fine guitar in 1966 in the same store. He smiled and said, yes, the owner. A stooped, grey-haired old gentleman came up, in suit, white shirt and tie, Senhor Emílio Fornetta. We all shook hands, and I proceeded to tell the story of buying my beautiful Di Giorgio Classic in December of 1966. He smiled, and laughed, "O senhor pegou um momento singular na empresa – uma economia horrível e ofertas que não vimos antes ou depois!" ["You experienced a singular memory at the store – a horrible economy and a sale that we had not seen before or have seem since."] I responded, telling him how I had saved every penny for six months living in a modest but colorful boarding house in Recife, all the time thinking of my dream of a Brazilian guitar and not even yet knowing of his shop. Only a classic guitar aficionado can share the experience and the pleasure of carefully picking up, holding, and then playing a fine instrument – the ease of fretting and best of all the incredible sound. I told Mr. Fornetta I had surely arrived in heaven that day! I had paid the cash I had saved in Recife for the best price and took the DiGiorgio home, its case cradled between my legs in a taxi (not risking the bus) to the house of my hosts who "guarded it" zealously for me for four months until I returned from travels in the interior to leave for the U.S. that next July.

He obviously was enjoying the reminiscing of the old days, and we soon had the customary "cafezinhos" brought to side tables. I went on to tell him of the battle I had with Pan Am to carry the guitar in its case on board and stow up front in a tiny compartment just behind the pilots' cabin and opposite the entry door, a place where the businessmen hung their suit jackets, the stewardess insisting it should go below in baggage. Emilio shrieked, "It would have cracked for sure. You were fortunate."

I then told him of the immense pleasure of playing the instrument the last almost twenty years, repairing it once when the lack of Brazilian humidity caused minor cracking up in Nebraska, and now the daily use of humidifiers. And that I had only one regret: There had been a Del Vecchio model, much more expensive and with better tone and even more beautiful than my DiGiorgio, but I simply could not afford it. He remembered all the guitars, models, types, all the details; he had relatives in São Paulo at all the guitar works – DiGiorgio, Giannini, and Del

Vecchio – and said, now knowing my name, "Miguel, you should be grateful. Times have changed."

"Senhor Fornetta, I confess I am not interested in a new guitar as we speak; this is a question of "matando saudades" [homesickness of old times] today, but maybe you have a "test" model I could play for you and my friend Flávio as well, to show what I've learned since 1966."

Flávio at that point began speaking to him in very fast but clear Italian, he listened and answered in the same parlance saying what a pleasure to see someone in Rio who really knows "our language." He pulled out a well – weathered case but inside an impeccably cared for Del Vecchio Rosewood guitar, rapidly checked the tuning and handed it to me. I in turned passed it to Flávio who took out a handkerchief, carefully placed it on the guitar where one's forearm rests and launched into a series of Bach, the Fugue in C, the famous Cello piece in D and then Scarlatti. (Customers and clerks were gathering around.) There was general applause and he handed it to me.

"I should have gone first; the 'sobremesa'" (Flávio) should have followed." I warmed up with the four simple exercises I had been doing for years, but then played two famous Heitor Villa – Lobos pieces from the "Estudos" and ended with an "ersatz" Malagueña. Resounding applause once again by the small crowd in the store. The guitar had wonderful tone, fretted beautifully, and the acoustics in the small room (well-planned long ago to sell guitars) made me sound better than I really was. Senhor Fornetta was beaming, saying it was wonderful to have his instrument being played by serious classic musicians and not just carioca "samba."

"You may come to my shop anytime, in fact, if we know ahead of time, I can invite some good friends and customers and perhaps advertise the event. Perhaps even today you made me a sale or two (in fact that happened, the clerks were in the process of helping out customers in the front of the shop). Miguel, in case you are interested, I have held back perhaps five or six of the guitars made by my friends in those years, and I think we could find one to suit your interests. *And,* improve for sure on the sound of your DiGiorgio. I am not sure if you are aware of it, so much time has passed, but that exact model you purchased became the favorite of the Bossa Nova professionals, including Baden Powell. But I have a classic that, pardon me, how do you say, 'Coloca – no na sombra.'" ["Puts it the shade!"]

"Senhor Fornetta, I had not planned on all this, but it certainly is a possibility. Owning two fine guitars is no sin. You always need a backup." (Senhor Fornetta laughed and retorted, "Just like beautiful women.") It reminds of the famous macho toast: "Here's to my wife and my lover. May they never meet!" I said, "I just returned to Rio after a long absence but will be here for the next two months or so and I will be back to take you up on your offer, at least of listening and trying out the guitar."

"Miguel, the last twenty years have been sad for those of us in the stringed instrument business. Imagine, *we* in Brazil have had to import rosewood from India and Ceylon, and some good mahogany from Mexico and Belize, but it's not the same, close, but not the same. The fine guitar makers, all in greater São Paulo, and all, incidentally, fine Italian – Brazilians, are up in years like me, but I'll be calling them to tell about this encounter and concert! Here's the business card; "parabens" on your playing and don't forget us!"

Flávio was beaming when we left the shop, "'Cara,' that was the most fun I've had with music since I got here. Porra! Professor, you have improved, heh heh, not as good as me, but improved. Now the second big surprise of the day, some real, acoustic Brazilian music and a fine dinner. There is a great café over in the back of Botafogo where they play real Brazilian 'chorinho,' and you and I shall take it in. It is probably the only place in this metropolis of five million people where you can actually listen to *quiet* music and converse between pieces. You can't even do that with classical music at Cecilia Meirelles Concert Hall!"

"Flávio, hey, I'm on your turf, I have not heard nor know much about 'chorinho,' but, clarinet, is it? And mandolin? I know Villa – Lobos wrote 'chorinhos' as well. Clue me in."

So that night we went to the "chorinhos" bar; on the bus I got the "short lecture" about "choros." Here's the gist of it. Carioca musicians in the 19th century came up with it mainly to entertain themselves. All acoustic, it was played at parties, pubs and the "botecos," and then on the radio, all before the "samba" craze really took over in Rio. Instruments were varied, but flute, guitar, cavaqunho (4 strings, somewhere between a mandolin and a ukulele in my mind), clarinet, maybe a saxophone and the only drum, a "pandeiro." It was truly Brazilian popular instrumental music and the most famous classic composer in all Brazil, Heitor Villa – Lobos called it according to one source, "The true incarnation of Brazilian soul." Flávio said it probably came from at least six popular forms like "maxixe," shottish, and others, and is really sophisticated stuff.

At the bar I guess we were hearing the continuation of that tradition. After my favorite dinner of salad, "bife" and fries and drinking altogether too much "choppe," the room quieted and four very gentlemanly fellows went up to the small stage, tuned their instruments and then lit into a blur of rapid, rhythmic, wonderful tunes. Flávio was a regular at the place, had met them all and informed me the quartet of middle-aged white "Cariocas" play strictly as a hobby (and I suppose for tips from the crowd). They all have daytime jobs. The performance was quiet: drum (is that an oxymoron?), clarinet, 'cavaquinho,' and mandolin. I can't repeat one song title, but it was quiet, entertaining, refreshing, and … uh … did get to be a bit tiring after a while.

Flávio and I spent most of the evening between songs and sets reminiscing, he telling more of his now four full years in Rio (I think there is a lot he is not telling), but mainly joking and doing his imitations of all the professors in the program back at Georgetown. The latter were hilarious, fit for any stand-up comedian, perfect parodies of language, gestures and demeanor. Flávio could do Argentinian, Brazilian, New York eastern, Chicago south side, Czechoslovakian, Spanish, Portuguese, all while satirizing literary criticism in the classes by stuffy, but well – intentioned eggheads. He said I was one of the most difficult – may I say "vanilla flavored" – the Nebraska accent or brogue is just that - but he managed to nail that as well. Gaherty in class, "Quiet, all of you, I'm going to say this just once, and in English because I want you to get it, so listen up!' Or something to that effect. A bit gruff like a drill sergeant.

He told me things I never knew about those student days, gossip and otherwise, and included some tales of wild endings to our Friday beer and pizza "Portuguese Club" events after classes. I would leave religiously after one hour, but the students carried on, sometimes closing the joint. And more than beer drinking took place. Ah, juventude! But Flávio said time and again how great the classes were and how Gaherty "turned us all on" to Brazil.

We took a taxi home, the colorful driver regaling us with stories of sex, politics, and corruption in Rio mainly told by his customers, including … uh … some congressmen and even Generals! Flávio and I agreed to stay in touch. I would have several research items to accomplish the coming week. I slept well with "chorinho" in my ears.

11

"HOME AGAIN" –
THE NORTHEASTERN FAIR
IN SÃO CRISTÓVÃO

Sunday, June 21. Waking up with just a slight headache but revived by Marcela's arrival with a hot thermos of "o estimulante de 10 centavos" as they used to call the "cafezinho" on the Recife billboards back in 1966 (thus creating demand for both coffee and sugar, the two main national agricultural products), it was time to hit it. I organized my briefcase with notepad and pen, made sure the camera had film and took the subway to downtown, getting off at Glória to meet Sebastião at his apartment. I've written of the northeastern fair so many times, it is difficult to recall the details, so I'll try to be brief.

We were on the Jardim de Allah – Jacaré Bus to the North Zone, and it was already full when we got on, mostly northeasterners, young men looking for a good time up at the fair, and some already drinking. When they saw us get on, one shouted, "O gringo pagará!" ["The gringo will pay!"] and they all laughed. Good thing Sebastião was with me, he whispered, "Just ignore them," and we took the last remaining two seats toward the front of the bus. The bus plodded along Rio Branco up to Avenida Getúlio Vargas, this because of the construction for the Rio Branco line of the metro. Once making the turn west and then north it got even worse, a real mess. The Avenida Getúlio Vargas on a good day was a disaster in process: 10 to 12 lanes of heavy traffic involving everything from VW taxis to the "stampede" of city buses, and worse, the phalanx of cargo trucks, all working their way to and from the North zone on down into commercial Rio. The traffic was far less this Sunday morning, but the construction made up for it.

The first view looking west was the hills on both sides west and north with "favelas," but somehow unreal, like a cubist painting, squares of all colors in the distance. You could see the Christ Statue through the fog and smog high up in the air on Corcovado to the west, and the sky was filled with the ubiquitous frigate birds. I never did figure out what those large birds lived on and really did not want to ask, but they were beautiful in flight. After the turn north and weaving through the residential streets of Meier we suddenly lurched to a stop and there it was, the old red brick Pavilion and on two sides all the "barracas" [sales stands] of the fair.

It was exciting at first, recalling I was first there in December 1966, and many times in the first months of 1967. I've written about it so many times that I can't recall it all, so maybe the reader will pardon me if I repeat some stuff. I think the last time was with Chico Buarque in 1970 a memorable moment when *I* for a change was his *cicerone* to something in Rio. Chico knew the "nordestino" reality well in São Paulo but had not been to São Cristóvão and waxed enthusiastic seeing all the "cordel" poems, so many reminding him of "Pedro Pedreiro." Those were the days that led to our collaboration on a research article comparing "Pedro Pedreiro" to the migration story – poems from the Northeast to Rio by the now "acclimatized" poets in Rio.

The Fair was perhaps bigger than I even remembered, a labyrinth of market stalls jammed next to each other seemingly without much order or planning, each just crying out for its own space. The main thing was the fair and the necessities it provided to the "nordestinos," clothing, hammocks, tools, and groceries: dried "charque, fumo de rolo," sacks of "farinha de mandioca," beans and rice. The air was pungent with food smells, most cooked over small charcoal stoves: meat on a stick, sit down cafes for a meal of sarapatel or feijoada, and then the beer stands and cachaça stands, the first still with the liter bottles of Brahma Choppe, the latter with at least ten flavors and variations of cachaça.

What seemed the same yet different was the noise level, always deafening in the past, but now, what's the word, crushing. It came from the music stands selling all manner of old cassete tapes, still older LP records, and the new CDs of northeastern music, mainly "forró" with Luís Gonzaga, all competing with each other, close by the cafés and tables and chairs where people were drinking beer and cachaça. I could scarcely hear Sebastião, having to get my ear next to his mouth when he was talking. He seemed used to the racket but used that derogative folklorist's term a time or two: the "de - characterization" of the Fair with all the damned noise.

Amazingly enough with all the "barulho" we still had a heyday with the "cordel" poets in their epic battle to compete with the noise and still sell their wares. I'll talk more eventually but my favorites and old standbys were still there – Azulão (João José dos Santos), Apolônio Alves dos Santos of the Guarabira connection, Gonçalo Ferreira da Silva, even old veteran Antônio Oliveira from the early days of the fair, and a relatively new – comer, some calling him a "penetra" ["gate crasher"] into the legitimate "cordel" scene, Raimundo Santa Helena.

All were happy to see me, but with the distractions we did not have any substantive conversations or revelations. Each had a similar story: with the end of AI – 5 in 1978, the past six years had been good for news and political story – poems, and they all had them. I purchased at least 5 to 10 from each poet and would practically pee my pants from the excitement of seeing all the great stuff to read and report on. Piecing it all together, they told of the political "abertura" ["opening"] in 1978 and 1979 and the flood of criticism and satire from "cordel" on the past twenty years of dictatorship, and especially the last two years of "Diretas Já" campaign, Dante de Oliveira, and the aftermath (1983 and now 1984). I would read them all in a quiet space, the Casa de Rui Library and Park, but later.

I spent all my cash, or almost all of it, on the story – poems, but begged Sebastião to have "almoço" at a northeastern version of the Carioca "churrascaria" dubbed "rodísio nordestino" in the big street beside the market. The famous "churrascaria" I had been to only once in the South Zone was in my memory, but I discovered this was a far more modest version, northeastern style, yet with all the accouterments. You sat down and got ready for an "over the top" Brazilian "almoço." I cannot begin to remember all the food, but there was an abundance. "Feijão e arroz, feijão nordestino, farofa," all kinds of cuts of pork, chicken and beef, including sausages, coming on the spits and carved by the waiters. But there also was a buffet with strictly northeastern dishes: "capivara, javali, sarapatel, angu a baiana, buchada de bode, carne de sol, aipim na manteiga" and northeastern vegetables and salads of all kinds. Sebastião tried a bit of everything, yours truly of the delicate stomach, just the ones I had remembered from the Northeast. And lots of icy Brahma Choppe to wash it down. I promised to pay my 50 cruzeiro novo part of the bill the next week at the Casa.

Just one note to finish the tale, I don't know if it is Brazilian (I think so) or just northeastern: the art of cleaning one's teeth after such a meal with toothpicks!

There is a standard joke in Brazil: in most restaurants there is a toothpick holder, round with a small hole in the center; you turn it upside down carefully and pull out a toothpick. "Gringos," yes, and even other foreigners mistake it for a saltshaker, and shake it vigorously in the middle of the meal; more than once I've seen toothpicks all over the table and floor. But there is more – the art of the toothpick!

I found this "social grace" to be one of the most hilarious of Brazilian customs of table etiquette over the years and confess to making a mental study of the phenomenon. I would imitate it in Portuguese classes back home. It's the eyes! One gets one's toothpick and carefully covers the mouth with the table napkin and then goes to work with the toothpick to do a thorough "policing of the area." I found myself watching their eyes as they performed the ritual, glancing from side to side, up and down, straight ahead, until it's all over, and neatly folding the napkin with toothpick inside before moving on perhaps to pay the bill (that's another matter, "o conto, a gorjeta," paying often with a personal check).

That day a gentleman outdid my highest expectations – he pulled out a roll of dental floss and performed that oblation as well, expertly, and efficiently I may add, moving the eyes just as though it were the toothpick routine. That however was the first and only time I had seen it.

I thanked Sebastião profusely, managed to get up from the table, very drowsy and wishing I were home for a long nap. Thinking of all this and both of us quite weary, we agreed to take a taxi home instead of waiting for the bus and the long ride back to Glória and then Copacabana. Before we got to the taxi stand there was a Carioca "happening" of sorts. What can you expect of two folklorists, one a legitimate Brazilian, the other a gringo "wannabe?" On the way to the taxi area there was an improvised "batucada" going on by many young men, all black in this case, the drumming on a drum or two but mainly on anything that makes noise – most observant visitors to Rio have seen this in the "botecos" or street bars. You take a spoon and keep the rhythm on knives, forks, spoons, coffee cups, beer glasses, and all seemed to be singing the latest "sambas." I quickly pulled out my camera wanting to document this great example of street life in Rio, asking Sebastião to hold my briefcase. (I think he had a hunch about what was just going to happen.)

One of the boys said, in colorful carioca slang mixed with some "palavrões," "Ó gringo filho da mãe, you take the picture, you pay! I want a round for all of us." There must have been at least a dozen guys in the group. I stammered that honestly, I was broke: "Estou liso, cara", had spent the last of my "cruzeiros" on stuff at the

Feira (they were not knowledgeable or interested in "cordel" broadsides). "I am just a tourist and wanted a photo of this great singing. And hey, I even had to borrow money from my friend for 'almoço.'" One said to the others, "You ever seen a broke gringo? (Much laughter) Come on, 'galego,' pay up."

Now I was sweating for sure. At about that time, one of the singers picked up an empty Brahma bottle, gave me a menacing look, stood up and began walking toward me, wobbling from the effects of all – morning beer drinking. Sebastião said, "Bora, Miguel, vamos dar o fora." ["Now! Miguel! Let's get the hell out of here"]. That was when the guy broke the bottle on the edge of the table and started to come toward us. Bedlam broke loose and someone yelled "Pega o bêbado, pega o bêbado." We must have been living right because a uniformed policeman came out of nowhere, grabbed the drunk's arm, twisted it making him drop the bottle and then twisted him to the ground. I thought the whole crowd would attack the policeman, but maybe from experience they knew better than to fool with the "macacos" or "fuzz." Bystanders had seen the whole thing so when the policeman asked us for explanation, they backed us up. The cop, I'm sure not wanting an obvious tourist in hot water, motioned us to go on, so Sebastião hailed a cab and 30 minutes later we are at his place in Glória. I thanked him profusely and said I'd see him at the Casa de Rui the next morning.

After getting off the bus on Princesa Isabel (Sebastião had loaned me the bus money), I made the walk home and collapsed into bed, still shaking a bit from the experience. Somehow or other I was able to take an hour's nap before getting up and showering and then pondering the morning's events. I will admit the thought crossed my mind of seeing the same "batucada" crowd next time in São Cristóvão but vowed to myself to not walk that direction (on the side street over near the "churrascaria") when leaving.

Sebastião and I would rehash the whole deal the next day. I was anxious to look at the "folhetos" bought that day but discovered they were mainly of very recent events, the "Diretas Já" campaign with a smattering of stories just before, all looking good but not filling in the gap from 1971 and the "Anistia completa" days. I was looking for the days of the mid 1970s with the Geisel administration, the end of AI – 5 in1978 and 1979 and the Figuereido regime which followed. I would ask Sebastião for tips and check the Casa's recent stuff.

I took that evenng to write a long letter to Molly filling her in on all the events of the past week and there were many. But mainly to let her know I was okay, and it looked like it would be great for research. I did mention the visit to the Ferreiras (she would be plenty curious to hear about that) and noting that Cristina Maria was now an ole' married lady with three kids. And I was careful to say I was safe in the streets and would be back at my old desk at the Casa de Rui tomorrow. Of course, asking for news of her and how was our Claire. Rui my landlord said mail service to the house was dependable, so I gave Molly that address for her letters, pleading her to write. An air mail letter took one week at most so there was time to write, and I promised to call sometime the next week.

That evening I took a deep breath and called Chico and Marieta, got him on the phone and both of us making plans for a visit to the house in the middle of next week. He was busy, now active again at the recording studio with a "whole pile of songs stocked up and backlogged from the old days."

12

MONDAY, MONDAY

June 22. Marcela was like clockwork with the café and abbreviated breakfast, this time with some sweet rolls bound to up the sugar high, and I was off at 9:00 on the bus to São Clemente and the walk up to the Casa de Rui. One funny encounter along the way, totally unusual for Rio and certainly for me. A rather good-looking carioca lady of about my age walking toward me on that crowded sidewalk suddenly called out, "Oi Arretado, faz tempo." ["Hi Cool Guy, it's been a while."] It was one of the girls from the Casa Library who knew me during the days of the Chico concert at the Niterói Bridge back in 1971, Clara her name. We talked just a minute, me saying I was heading right now for the library, she on an errand but would see me there later. She asked me if I remembered her saying "I'm next" at the big shindig in the Salão Nobre at the Casa after the Philology Congress? She smiled, winked, and said Claudia might be waiting for me. I think I turned a bit red, couldn't think of a proper retort and just said, "Great to see old friends. See you in a while." I had put Claudia out of my mind but just then remembered her talk of a "dinner date." Uh oh.

In the research center there was a quick reunion with Sebastião who admitted maybe we had dodged a bullet yesterday, but was smiling, and said, "Remember Guimarães Rosa, 'Viver é muito perigoso!' ["Living is very dangerous"] Just another day in Rio." He laughed. I remembered the whole deal including my borrowed cruzeiros, got out my billfold and paid Sebastião my debt from the restaurant, busses and some extra. He tried to not accept it, a very Brazilian gesture, but I know he would have missed it. We turned to the business at hand, me telling the titles I bought yesterday, mostly of "Diretas Já", he helping me to fill in the gaps from the Casa's recent additions (no one knew it like he). It got interesting for research and for "Letters" to Hansen and Iverson.

There was a whole slew of story – poems, and with the new "system" of the library (incredibly expanded and far more efficient now in the new Research Center) plus my past work, good reputation, and let's face it, connections, they were brought to the table for my perusal and a quick reading. The best thing is I could then send them to the new xerox machine for copying. I could pick them up the next day, paying a reasonable fee (xerox was incredibly expensive in the streets) and take them home safely tucked in my briefcase.

A very Brazilian thing: no matter what the job or rank, menial to magnificent, Brazilians are zealous in protecting their own turf. I learned that Roberto the young man hired just to run the Xerox machine was indeed the "manda - chuva" in his own domain and you had to be nice and hopefully never in a hurry (I slipped him a nice tip after each session, against the rules, but both of us saying it was for extra "paper.") But it reminded me of a great encounter, time before in downtown Rio.

I was with old friend Caetano Forti at his office building in downtown Rio where he was working at that time as a stockbroker, so it was an upscale office building, except for one thing. The passenger elevator is what I imagined you might run into in an old skyscraper in New York City: large, with mirrors on three sides, brass railings, and the control panel including a large wheel with a handle that ran the thing, all this you saw on one side when you walked in. Oh yes, and a small stool that folded out of the wall for HIM! The elevator "boy" was an aged gentlemen in the livery of a long-time veteran of the job including braid on his shoulders and the round cap he wore, anachronisms of another age. He knew the names of all the employees who "saluted" him such as "Mestre Roberto," did not have to ask for the floors because he knew them all and was given the courtesy of an "obrigado, Mestre" at the end of the ride. Caetano simply said after we got out on the proper floor: "Não mexa com Mestre Roberto, e mais que tudo, não fique sozinho no elevador com ele! É de arrepiar!" ["Don't mess with Master Roberto, and more than anything else, don't end up alone in the elevator with him. It's scary!"] And he laughed.

Luís Fernando Veríssimo my favorite Brazilian writer of that time wrote a "chronicle" that could have been about the same "mestre", and my new friend Roberto do Xerox wasn't anything less.

My mouth watered just looking at the titles spread on the long table before me with Sebastião looking on across from me, each important for research and "Letters."

Debate da Arena com o MDB. Abraão Batista
MDB Derrota ARENA, o Grande Duelo do Povo em Contra os Seus Exploradores.
Delfim. O Pacote. Azulão
Delfim Deu Fim ao Brasil. Gonçalo Ferreira da Silva
A Saída do Presidente Médici e a Posse de Geisel. 1974
Só Geisel Criou o Momento do Pobre Participar em ... 1974
O Dragão do Fim da Era. Rodolfo Coelho Cavalcante. 1975
O Movimento Estudantil e as Duchas Erasmo em São Paulo. 1977
Feitos da Revolução. José Soares, 1977
"Cordel pela Anistia Ampla, Geral e Irrestrita."
Anistia Ampla e a Volta de Arraes. 1979
Os Ex – Exilados e os Desaparecidos.
A Guerra contra a Ditadura – Brizola
Política, Inflação e Carestia. RCC

"Meus Deus! Uma mina de 'cordel.'" ["My God, a 'cordel gold mine."] Plus, there as well were four or five "folhetos" on the new upcoming national hero, Lula of the steel workers, the strikes, the imprisonment. And the feeble efforts of General Figueiredo to stop it all. All this was exactly what I had missed out on being absent from Brazil for research since 1971. These story – poems would fill those gaps. I would discover that the current poets in São Cristóvão plus Franklin Maxado from São Paulo could and would fill me on the entire "Diretas Já" campaign which came after them. It was all a huge order but had to get done by the end of August and travel back home. I had, as we say back home, "a full plate," and that was just "cordel."

Sebastião, myself and a couple other of the interns had lunch across the street at the same old "Prato do Dia" café. It was "basic Brazilian:" "frango grelhado, arroz e feijão, salada de legumes, batata frita e uma fatia de doce para sobremesa," all small but filling portions. Guaraná or Coca Cola to drink. Lots of laughter, gossip of goings – on at the Research Center, but mainly I had a chance to get more details of Sebastião's background and life. One of the many sons of Francisco das Chagas

Batista famous "cordel" poet, printer and colleague of Leandro Gomes de Barros, he was perfect for the Casa de Rui library and "cordel" collection. Most of what I remember was told informally in chatting while perusing the "cordel" collection over many days, months and years.

He was modest to the extreme and one of the nicest persons I ever met, I think perhaps one of my favorite Brazilians, and that is saying something! The guidance he gave me, almost spoon fed at times, from details on Leandro Gomes de Barros, Sebastião's father Chagas Batista, brother Pedro Batista, Rodolfo Cavalcante, or Cuíca de Santo Amaro was invaluable. And he knew more about the greatest "cantadores" of the Northeast mainly because some came from his family.

Talk about genetics and genes – he had it all. Most important were the details, clarifications, and answers to questions I would have as I read the "cordel" collection. And, in between, details on his life. I never wrote them down. I guess I never imagined it would end. Sebastião died, if I have the tale and memory correct, like we say in Nebraska, "with his boots on," collapsing while giving a talk on "cordel" at a conference in the Northeast. Just some memories for now – Sebastião told of years it took for him to gradually migrate from Paraíba down to Rio first working for the railroad and experiencing a real encounter with "cangaceiros," [northeastern bandits] then with a major stop in Bahia. He became a "veterinarian" without the degree due to incredible knowledge of animals and practiced in that state (I provide a disclaimer: this memory is fuzzy, and I may not have it right). Another, and I do remember clearly: from the very beginnings when he arrived in Rio de Janeiro, he frequented the places where "Nordestinos" hung out, first at the "Estação Central" train station where he became the "homem das cartas," beating out letters on a tiny manual typewriter for illiterate northeasterners homesick for home and wanting to write to girlfriends and wives and mothers. He took this skill to São Cristóvão later to the Fair. But for most, it was his personal, encyclopedic knowledge of "cordel" that was foremost. I should have dropped everything and done a book on him. Naïve! "Ingênuo!"

Sebastião for years went to night school and through some pistolão ["pull"] of Professor Thiers was admitted to university where he studied for a Brazilian Literature Degree. He had worked for years as well at the Ministry of Agriculture and was officially retired; the minute pension I surmise scarcely helped pay for the education. Finally, he did receive the degree and the added prestige it gave him at the Casa.

Most unusual were two other unrelated events: Sebastião could see I was lonely at times in Rio and often tried to get me to go with him to a "gafieira" or public dance hall, thinking it would be easy to meet women there. For more naïve reasons, mainly because of Catholic upbringing, I was fearful and desisted. He insisted the women were of good "virtue" and did not have to worry about that. But my religion did not keep me from going to "Umbanda" in an old, dilapidated Flamengo mansion with Sebastião, an event I'll tell in a while. Suffice to say for now, you never but never expected an intellectual of the pedigree and quality of Sebastião to be an "umbandista." Stranger things have happened in Brazil.

Back to that lunch. One of the interns, a young, handsome fellow from Minas Gerais, chided me, saying "Miguel, you must be exhausted." "Why?" I asked. "Pois, a rich gringo, good looking, unattached (he did not know I was married and with a daughter), alone in Rio!" And he bent over laughing. I said, "Não senhor, infelizmente."

49

13

An Unlucky Number? Cláudia

That brings me to tell what happened that afternoon back in the library. You may have guessed it – Cláudia!

I had remembered our initial short conversation a few days before. I popped my head into her office, she gave me that sign of being on the phone but to wait, so I did. She got up, came over, gave me a big embrace (uh oh) and things went from there. "So, you haven't forgotten about our drinks and dinner? No time like the present; why not tonight at the café on top of the Othon. I'll meet you there at 8:00"

"Cláudia, you have to know I'm on a fairly modest budget and am afraid that high end place might not fit it."

"Não se preocupe, I've got friends in the management, and we will be treated fine, in fact, old buddy, dinner's on me!"

I did the bus home, showered and cleaned up, put on dress slacks, nice shoes, nice sport dress shirt and got the Avenida Jardineira mini – bus to the Othon. Elevator up to the top floor with the café, dance floor and incredible view of Copacabana, I took a seat at the bar, ordered a caipirinha and enjoyed the scenery. This is a high – class place, so the music is soft (for Brazil), a late Bossa – Nova type for cocktails and early dinners. A band starts (we would find out) at 9:00. Oh, for the curious reader, I was wearing my wedding band, not that *that* makes much difference in Rio.

At about ten after eight Claudia came out of the elevator and the sight was enough to make you do at least one double take – this is the beauty the Brazilians brag about! A tight waistless (is that the right word?) top, short skirt revealing tanned legs, impeccable makeup, and hair, long and straight in the current carioca style. She saw me, came over, did the embrace and light kiss on the lips, and called for the maître whom she seemed to know well. We were ushered to a quiet table on the side yet with the terrific view, I brought my unfinished caipirinha with me to the table and she ordered a glass of white wine.

"Just friends," she said, "we'll see," and laughed. I think it was then that I first thought, "Okay, Gaherty, this is not going to be easy." She looked me in the eyes, took my hand and said, "You have not forgotten how well we got along last time have you? We both are a few years older, but I don't think bad for wear, hein? I know I've worked like hell to stay in shape, what do you think?" She leaned a bit forward as she said that, smiled and showed enough of that adequate decolletage of times passed. Uh oh. It did not help when she moved her hand from the table and just placed it on my thigh. Hi Ho Silver!

"Claudia, all true, all true, but you seem to be forgetting that minor detail I already mentioned the other day."

"Oh, *that*. I understand, Mike. Let's catch up on thirteen years, huh? You go first."

Relieved to just be talking, I told Claudia basically what the reader knows if they read "Letters from Brazil II and III." Not being able to do research in Brazil, I had fallen into the good luck of being a cultural speaker on Adventure Travel's flagship the "International Adventurer" and done no less than five trips with them, all during summers away from the university or on academic leave. I told of girlfriend Amy from those days, how we were almost married! And then how I got back together with first love Molly in Washington D.C., reconciled, renewed the friendship and romance, and married and we now had a wonderful daughter. And now the big step to move to D.C. teach at Georgetown and back here to do "Letters IV."

Claudia listened, nodded her head a few times, smiled, and said, "You seem very happy. I'm glad for you. My story is not quite the same."

"Pois, that's what I'm waiting to hear." We both refreshed the drinks, and she gave me the "short" version.

"Miguel, things have been interesting. I guess you must be surprised I'm still at the Casa de Rui, but I'll get around to that. It was later that same year you had to leave Brazil, the Merzog business and Chico's 'turné.' All the girls at the Casa kept close track of that, after all, 'Arretado' was a regular at the Research Center!

And other reasons! (She patted my leg under the table.) I ended up dating one of my former professors from the P.U.C. He taught Brazilian Literature and did some writing of his own, but his family was, what do you say, "well – heeled," importing wines from Europe and exporting tobacco and chocolate from Brazil. You might have even heard the family name, Schmidt, from Rio Grande do Sul. It was easy to turn my head; he was wonderful looking, intelligent, suave, the right pedigree at the P.U.C. and with no limit to possibilities outside the stodgy university. And soon enough, good in bed, but maybe not quite as good as you! Ha ha. He was older, five years to be exact.

"The family kept urging him to leave academia and join the company, so he gave it a try, inviting me along on two or three 'business' trips to Paris, Madrid, and Lisbon. It became a whirlwind romance, how could it not? I don't think any normal girl could be wined and dined and with all that culture and not be impressed. We married a year later in 1972. Life was good, a beautiful home in the Barra, a condo in Salvador, and another in Porto Alegre. I took a leave from the Casa and lived that good life for about five years. But Oscar, as it turns out, like most Brazilian men, had a roving eye, and I discovered it almost accidentally when I returned unexpectedly to the house from a visit to my family in Minas. Imagina! The nerve of the bastard. He was shacking up with some beauty from the Rio office in *our* bedroom in the Barra!

"Fortunately, I never had gotten pregnant (we took precautions from the very beginning), both of us saying there would be time for that soon. When we did begin to try, no luck and endless doctors, tests and examinations for both of us. That was when he began to mess around. You may remember me telling you that last time, when I was still in school in Minas, the same thing. I could not put up with being the faithful wife while hubby was having fun on the side. The divorce was uncontested, and I guess you could say, I was well rewarded for my time, very well rewarded. I have no financial worries. Miguel, it does not make up for lost love."

I looked into her eyes, moist they were, and patted her hand saying, "I'm sorry Claudia, so sorry."

"So, that was eight years ago, I don't know if I am over it yet. When I heard you were coming back, my heart beat faster for a moment, what do you call it, maybe it would be 'a stab in the dark?' Not too funny, huh? That was before I learned from Orígenes you were now married with a family. I guess I had hoped against hope we could renew that spark. It was good, wasn't it? Anyway, the Casa took me back and it still *is* the most prestigious Library in Brazil, save that of USP or Joseph Mindlin's in São Paulo, and I can use their paltry salary for cigarette money. Ha. Ha. There have been several men, one even lasting up to a year, but porra – no spark!"

Gaherty generally is not at a loss for words, the opposite, and sometimes I am impulsive, uh, to a fault. But just then I truly was at a loss for words. It flashed through my mind, how many men, including married men, would jump at this chance? Most I knew. And that included colleagues at Georgetown, no place no more Catholic. But, er, like the old Jesuits, pragmatic. You will never know what saved me, not in a million years. As I was sincerely trying to think of words to comfort Claudia, another image and voice from the past came up to the table.

"Gaherty you cafajeste! This is surely poetic justice. I cannot imagine what double dealing crap you are feeding this beautiful woman! Is she as good a "foda" as I was? Oh, by the way, hi Claudia. (Both were looking daggers at each other, maybe for a good reason I'll explain later.) Miguel, last time I heard, you were back with your childhood sweetheart or some merda like that. I would have flown to San Francisco like we planned, porra, I would have flown to the *moon* to have us together again. You have no idea of the heartbreak you caused, damned near a mental breakdown!"

Pause the projector. I ask, how many times in your life are you caught between what must be two of the world's most beautiful and sexy women, and like … who the hell was that French guy, Camus? Sarte? "No Exit?" I don't know why that flashed through my mind, I am not a fan of French, French Literature and French philosophers, and for sure never read any of it. This is not good writing, but I have to do an "aside" and explain to you the reader.

If you read "Letters III" you know about the second woman, but that puts you in a very special and may I say, miniscule club. Sônia was another … uh … sexy chapter from back in 1971. She started it all, but I did not resist, that is, until later. She was one of the "how about me next time" girls from the library at the Casa de Rui. We had some steamy get togethers, two of them right here at the Othon, another at the family's luxury condo in the Barra, and how can I say this? If I had wanted to marry Sônia, have a Brazilian, even an international life of luxury and maybe an important diplomatic post like Cultural Attaché to Brazil, she and her incredibly rich and powerful Brazilian family would have made it happen. She was partially right about San Francisco; we had talked of a "rendezvous" that Fall, but there never was a promise or commitment on my part. She called me in Lincoln talking of it, I said I had smoothed things over with Molly, and no, and she blew up. Sônia, by the way, is one fiery lady in case you haven't figured it out yet.

I'll repeat from "Letters III:" a helluva lot of people would have thought I was crazy to turn all that down. As I told her, and it's still true, there was no way with my upbringing on a modest farm in Nebraska, porra, my whole background and life, that I could have done that. That's why it's Professor Gaherty now from Georgetown, married to Molly and with a dear daughter, Claire. And I thought of them both just then.

"Claudia, we've met and talked about this two – timer, and *I* thought we were on the same page, after all, what is it? 'May the best girl win?' Ha! So, I'm really surprised to see this." She sat down at one of the chairs at our table, fuming, waiting for an explanation from one or the both of us. I think ears had perked up at most of the adjoining tables, but "Porra! que se pode fazer?" ["Crap! What can you do?"] Claudia spoke first.

"Sônia, if it will make you feel any better, I was the one who invited Mike up here, all pretty innocent (I wish it were otherwise), sharing each other's lives since 1971. Nothing more than that. And we were making progress each telling his or her story and having a good time. 'Beleza,' the *best* girl did win and she's in Washington, D.C. I can live with that, and I don' know and could care less whether you can."

You could see the wheels turning in Sônia's head, with her fiery and impulsive temperament, trying to digest the last ten minutes but still capable of making a scene. She turned those blazing eyes to me and just said,

> "Pois, senhor 'family man,' the way I figure it, you owe me one. Unless you want a very unpleasant and I dare say embarrassing scene here and right now, remember, my family owns a good part of the Othon, will you agree to meet me right here, same time, same place, next Saturday night? Maybe like Cláudia, we can just have a 'chat' about old times. I promise I won't bring my father or any of his bodyguards, or my husband for that matter. How about it? 8:00 p.m. Saturday?"

I looked at Cláudia, she nodded her head just slightly, on the verge of tears. "Okay, to avoid the scene and God knows you are the one capable of that, you're on. One proviso – let Cláudia and I finish our evening."

"Oh, I already have an idea how that's going to end. See you Saturday." She gave a perfunctory nod and said a quick goodbye to Cláudia, walked over to the elevator and was gone.

I think we both took a deep breath and I said, "Let's have another caipirinha, maybe a double, finish our conversation, and I'll take you home. Topa?"

I think she was trying to control her own emotions, also avoid a scene and maybe, just maybe, had more to say, especially considering events. "Miguel, maybe this has been a mistake, a big mistake. I'm sorry I put you through it. Embarrassing for both of us. I've heard you and listened to you. I know I'll be seeing you at the Casa, we can't avoid that. But maybe we can, just maybe, be friends for these few weeks, nossa, even go to the beach once or twice, or if not, at least to a nice place for dinner."

"Claudia, thank you. I think it's a good solution. I'll be in and out of the library often; let's do that "prato do dia" with Sebastião and maybe even Orígenes. I'm sure it will cheer us all up. Now, I've got an idea. Are you hungry yet? All of a sudden, I am. My old hangout "O Braseiro" is just a couple of blocks away. We can have a Gaherty bachelor style dinner there and then I'll get you a taxi for a ride home."

She stood up, said, "I'll take a rain check on that, no appetite Mike. Just Give me a nice hug and walk me to the lobby; they will hail a taxi for me. By the way, I've got a lovely apartment on the curve of Flamengo, I think perhaps the same building you were in with the Fortis way back when. I have a terrific cook, left over from the Schmidt days and we can do you a real 'Gaúcho churrasco;' I won't say I had not hoped for something else to happen this evening, but I know a lot about spoiled marriages, and I'll be damned if I cause one."

That was how it turned out, she getting into a cab at the front door, me doing the short walk to the "Braseiro," "matando saudades" for that great sit – down food from the bar stool. You may say, "How in the hell can you have an appetite now?" Sometimes food and drink can heal all. Sometimes. Oh, one detail. Heitor Dias joined me. He had been waiting in his car parked at the side entrance of the Othon and waved me over the minute I walked out the door. He said, "Arretado, you look like you need some company. We had a guy up in the bar and he told me all about that tiff you just had with Sônia Rodrigues. Look out, my friend, that one has a reputation! (He knew about 1971 as well.)"

"Heitor, I'm hungry and headed to the 'Braseiro,' can you eat a bite?"

"Amigo, the question is when can I *not* eat a bite. 'Bora. My driver will pick me up, let's see, in an hour and a half, okay?"

It was busy as usual that time of night, but after just a ten-minute wait or so while we drank the first of icy Brahmas, we got the bar stools on the side with a view of the street. I had the old favorite: "filê, arroz a grego, vinagrette, fritas" and another beer. Heitor did that and a little more. It was too public to talk of anything too private, but he did say in general that the DOPS is aware of a lot of street activity, still "hangover" or "ressacca" of the failure of Dante Oliveira, but that most of the action is going on behind the scenes with the politicians in Brasília, a real hotbed of pro and con he can't even figure out. We finished and he offered to take me home saying, "Arretado, gringos are 'filet – mignon' to the pickpockets and muggers on Copacabana Beach, especially at night." I said I would take the chance, so he shrugged his shoulders, reluctantly agreed, but said he would have a man in an unmarked car along the way. "No way my main gringo person of interest is going to get mugged on my duty." He laughed, gave me an abraço and sped off in his staff car.

So I did the long walk back on the beach "calçada" to Leme, much needed to both calm down and digest the ups and downs of the last few hours. It took about a quarter of the walk back to Leme, but it worked. Calm and married virtue intact. Whew.

There was a phone message that night. Flávio had called. He has to go to Buenos Aires for one month, command performance. His English Textbook Publisher has a possible contract to do the same entire series already done in Brazil, but now in Buenos Aires; Flávio is perfect for the job with Italian, Spanish, Portuguese, and English. They will be working out all the preliminaries for maybe a one-year contract, and he's excited. He said he would see me in August.

Tchao.

14

⌒⌒

CASA DE RUI "FOLHETO" RESEARCH

So the next day it was all business back at the Casa de Rui. Sebastião had begun digging up the titles we already had talked about, and now I could begin filling in the blanks on politics and all since 1971.

One of the first was by a minor poet all the way from Campo Grande Piaui, Cunha Neto, "A Saída do Présidente Médici e a Posse do Novo Presidente Ernesto Geisel." ["The Exit of President Médici and the Inauguration of New President Ernesto Geisel"] Another was "Só Geisel Criou este Direito do Pobre Velho Participar no Pão," ["Only Geisel Created the Right of the Poor Elderly to Participate in the Bread"] de Antônio Batista Romão of Juazeiro do Norte. Both express the usual optimism of the poets of "cordel" for a new president, in this case from 1974 to 1979. Shortly after he came in there was a positive announcement for politics: the military would permit elections for mayors and governors in the Fall of 1978. The MDB is expected to do well. But presidential elections will still be indirect, and General Figueiredo will be the man.

José Soares of Pernambuco registered in "cordel" "The Victory of ARENA" of November 15, 1974, treating it all like it were a soccer match, a recurrent topic in "cordel," and a happy one because the government approved of this type of distraction for the masses (recall 1970 and President General Geisel and his transistor radio at the World Cup in Mexico):

Iniciou-se a Partida	The match began
Um jogava, outro jogava	One good play, another good play
A Arena fazia um gol	Arena made a goal
MDB empatava…	MDB tied it up …

The final score: ARENA won 75 mayoral posts in the State of Pernambuco, MDB 9, ARENA elected 11 "vereadores" [alderman], MDB 10. MDB did come out well in São Paulo and Rio, a sign of things to come, but the poet affirms that "Geisel was happy" with the results. No ominous signs on the horizon yet.

A much more ominous "cordel" poem the next year by Rodolfo Coelho Cavalcante was "The Dragon at the End of Time" ["O Dragão do Fim da Era"]; he excoriated the evils of International Communism, according to him, responsible for what was going on in Brazil. I paraphrase:

"They rob banks and more banks with arms in their hands. They kill employees who earn their daily bread there. They rob brazenly with their only desire of making a revolution."

"They kidnap ambassadors, putting the Nation in danger, demanding enormous ransoms. Our country is indeed going through a bad time due to this Dragon." (p.3.)

The poets ends with his own plan:

We will not cross our arms
Against this vile Monster
That opposes Liberty
With its thousands of lies … (p.4)

That however was one of the few defenses of the Military, no surprise under the circumstances, i.e. Rodolfo's near death at the hand of thugs hired by Communist politicians in his home state of Alagoas in the 1940s or 1950s. The poet narrowly escaped death by drowning and the rest of his life railed against Communism.

Sebastião filled me in on the nitty – gritty of those days, "difficult times," noting that after the end of Censorship the "cordel" played a major role in educating its own public of the sorrowful events since 1964. The students, silenced by the government in a crackdown on the UNE since 1965 and AI 5, reacted in their own way with "pseudo – cordel," in effect, mimeographed and xeroxed story – poems using the "cordel" format to criticize the government. Just one, discovered in the collection at the Casa de Rui makes their case: "The Student Movement and the Erasmo Cold Showers in São Paulo" ["O Movimento Estudantil e as Duchas Erasmo em São Paulo"] in 1977.

The theme was one of the battles between the students and the government initiated by a protest in April of 1977 against the budget cuts for the universities and the rise in price of meals served in the cafeterias of the schools. A protest letter achieved no results, so the students went to the streets where the police of Secretary of Public Safety Chief Erasmo Dias awaited them with tear gas. Seeing all the smoke the students sat down *en masse* on the Viaduto do Chá and read their letter of protest one more time, now adding other exigencies: stop inflation and give amnesty to political prisoners. All ended in peace that day, workers in the skyscrapers of Líbero Badaró Avenue throwing confetti down to the streets.

The next day was different (according to the student poet). In the Largo de São Francisco the students were met by federal police and the local "brucutus" ["neanderthals"]. The violence began with a "quebra – pau muito feio" ["a really ugly scene of beatings"] in which "no sanduíche da polícia, estudante era recheio." ["in the cops' sandwiches, students were the mayo"]. There were "porradas à revelia" ["no end of belly club knocks"] and to cool the students' remaining enthusiasm, it all ended with "banho de água fria"" ["a bath of cold water"].

Apesar da polícia ter	In spite of the police having
Distribuido muita pancada	Given out a lot of beatings
Essa manifestação	That manifestation
Foi higiênica e asseada …	Was both hygienic and clean …

Everyone was soaked! The story – poem ends with rhetoric unfamiliar to "cordel:" "I won't go on long; I'll contain my enthusiasm. Since all masturbation must end in orgasm. The students are now traumatized from taking Erasmo's showers." But it is its ending that sends chills: "I wrote this 'folheto' using my imagination, and if for some reason I end up in prison, please put my name on the Open Letter from the population." In one sense this "pseudo – cordel" by a student who lived the times, summarizes ten years: the first protests in 1966, 1967 and 1968; the student protests of 1970; the marches and protests of the labor unions in 1979, 1980 and 1981. All would end with the "euphoria" of "Diretas Já" ["Direct Elections Now"] to come.

Time was going on that day, I had lunch with Sebastião with promises to be back tomorrow and went out the Research Center stairway, not going down to the library, not yet ready to meet Cláudia. Another meeting was long overdue: Chico Buarque, Marieta and the kids. I called from the Casa de Rui and was told anytime after three was okay. Topo!

15

❦

ESTÁ NA HORA!

["IT'S ABOUT TIME!"]

After I got out of the taxi and rang the buzzer at the outside gate, I could hear a commotion inside, Chico yelling to someone, "O,' o Arretado está aqui. Esconde o ouro e as joias e as fitas novas. Gringo na área," ["Uh oh. Arretado is here. Hide the family jewels and gold and the new tapes. Gringo in the goal area"] and a peal of laughter. He and Marieta came out to the gate, big hugs and immediately ushered me into the airy and expansive living room, Chico calling to the maid for "cachaça e Brahma," with little protest by me. The kids were now in "colégio" and would be home later. We settled down to a wonderful afternoon session of basically catching up.

Chico insisted that I go first, so I repeated what the reader already knows: married to Molly, daughter Claire, Associate Professor at Georgetown, and now back to Brazil legally (we laughed) for "Letters IV." Reporting on the day to day, economics, politics, and catching up on "cordel" for a new book.

Their turn. They reminisced and reminded of our last time together on "International Explorer" in 1977 in Lisbon and thanked me again. "Oh, what happened to Amy? We thought for sure she had a ring on your finger and another through your nose!" I answered, saying, basically it was she that ended it all, am not positive yet exactly why, but still with "greener pasture" for International Travel, but all turned out fine with my true love Molly. Marieta said, "She must be something to have caught you 'Arretado,' you are like a 'marujo' ['sailor'] with a girl in every port." Chico just glanced at me and winked. I pulled out the small packet of

61

wedding pictures plus two or three of young Claire, they looked, smiled, and agreed that indeed the Gahertys were a terrific family.

Another round of drinks and we got into their story. Basically, there were very rough times until the end of AI – 5 and censorship but a real "renacimento" ["renaissance"] now since 79' – lots of new songs recorded that had been in the "gaveta," ["drawer"] and best of all new shows, turnés [tours] all over the country. "Not like in those innocent, heady days of 1965, 1966 and 1967, but good, steady income and a new reality in Brazil. 'Arretado,' even though Dante de Oliveira failed, the tide has turned; we are all confident Tancredo Neves will win in the indirect come next January. My family knows Maluf, an old product of the conservative machine in São Paulo, and he doesn't stand a chance to the wave of popularity Tancredo has in the entire nation. Let's drink to that!"

I asked about songs and Chico reviewed some of the highlights, "Milagre Brasileiro" ["The Brazilian Miracle"] in 1975, "Meu Caro Amigo" ["To My Dear Friend"] in 1976, "Pivete" ["Street Urchins"] in 1978, and of course I knew "Tanto Mar" ["So Much Ocean"] in 1977. "There are many more, many really you might not either want to or need to know about, some love songs, and a big success with 'Ópera do Malandro' ['The Rogue's Opera'] in 1981. And I've been writing books, two novels and another on the way. The sales are miniscule, folks say too intellectual, I guess carrying on like Dad and Uncle Aurélio, but it has been fun and a big distraction from old stuff. Don't you ever get tired of 'cordel' and all that?"

I said, "Well, I've really had an unwanted break from that since 1971, but porra, teaching Brazilian Portuguese and culture is my job. Despite the 'Redentora' ['Redeemer'] I still love the country, and of course, you sure provided lots of unexpected fun with the old LP and concerts before my uh unexpected departure! And like you, 'cordel' has been on a roll since 1979 and the end of AI – 5, lots of new stuff I'm finding at the Casa de Rui and also up at São Cristóvão."

"É. Certo. ["Right. True.] Oh, I have to apologize; I never did get to that sequel of 'Pedro Pedreiro' but I've got one you'll love, from our hiking days up to the Vista Chinesa, 'Passaredo.' ['Passing of the Birds']. You got to get out your bird book to appreciate it though." He laughed and laughed.

"Miguel, I think there is just one song so far this year that may hit you between the eyes, it's called 'Pelas Tabelas' ['Banging Pots and Pans']. I'll give you all the tapes and if you don't have a recorder, one of those too. Maybe we can talk later about it all. Hey, I want to get back up to Vista Chinesa sometime this week, why don't you come along, I'll grab a small bird book and you'll see what we missed last time."

Marieta came in the room saying I am bound to stay for a late dinner or early supper. The beer had begun to hit me by then and what I really needed was a nap, but hey, bobo, [dummy], you may not get this chance again for a while. I took a deep breath and asked about Cristina Maria, Marieta laughed and said, "You mean that chick you let get away! She's happily married, has three wonderful children and I don't know how she manages it, good nannies I guess, is a crackerjack lawyer along with Sebastião in the firm. Why didn't you two ever get serious anyway?"

I said, "We did Marieta, me more than her, but what killed it all was she was not about to go live in the United States, and I couldn't imagine making a living in Brazil. It's a long story. I do think I should call her just for old times, no shenanigans, but just a bit of reminiscing and catching up. If we need a chaperone, are you and Chico available? Ha ha ha."

"I would think you would want it a little more private than that. But she's no dummy; she'll think of something that won't upset the applecart at home."

Dinner was great, all my favorite Brazilian foods including a shrimp soufflé and a "bife com fritas" ["steak and fries"] and a too rich "brigadeiro" chocolate for dessert. They wanted to know things about the U.S., how the Vietnam morass had finally died down and how was living in Washington, D.C. Chico respects the U.S., wishes it well, but is no friend of its Latin American policies dating way back to Fidel in 1959. But that reminded him of our music, the Rock 'n Roll and the concerts. "Porra! We were on a roll until Merzog. Hey, I'm doing a concert in the Maracanazinho two weeks from now, are you up to coming, first row seats, and coming up on stage to sing a couple of rock songs?" His face lit up with a big smile and he laughed thinking of it all.

"I dunno. It's been a long time, but that will all come back easily enough. But do you remember my request from 1971? My all-time favorite Brazilian song and the only one I can really do, 'Manhã de Carnaval?' ["Carnival Morning"]. If I could do something about nerves and stage fright it would be an all-time dream come true."

"O' Arretado, we in the business have things for that; 'erva' ['weed'] has come a long way as a 'calmante' ['tranquilizer']. And if you stumble, which I doubt, Ginni, I and the band will finish it, better yet we should all plan on that, the 'bis' second time around. And the instrumental background. My guitarist Adalfo can make it all sound like a dream."

"I'm thinking follow it with the original movie clip of the end of the film, Orféu carrying Euridice up Babilônia Hill, the denouement and the kids dancing. Can we swing that?"

"Yes, for sure, and I've got a new song I'm working on to end it all after that. A secret for now. Hey, Miguel, it is so good you are back; we are coming to the end of the nightmare. "O Brasil já é outro! O', que tal a caminhata na manhã de quinta – feira, saindo aqui de casa as 9 horas?" ["Brazil now is another place. How about a hike Thursday moring, leaving the house here at 9:00 a.m.?"]

"Certo, vou aparecer com a máquina fotografica e você proveera' o livro sobre os pássaros e um bom binóculo? Pode ser?"

["For sure. I'll arrive with my camera, and you can bring a bird book and good binoculars. How about that?"]

"Combinado amigo. Até a quinta."

["Agreed my friend. See you Thursday."]

16

More "Literatura De Cordel"

The next morning it was back to the "Casa de Rui" for another "cordel" session. But I took a deep breath before getting on the bus and made a call to Maria Aparecida at the number she had written on that slip of paper at the "Castelo" ["House of Prostitution"] in Flamengo days earlier, her place of work. I don't know yet if it was to her office or what, but she answered in what I would call her "business" voice, so it must have been to the Castelo. We spoke just a moment or two but decided to meet for a late lunch (2:00 p.m.) at a yet unmentioned place; she said she would pick me up in her blue VW sedan in front of the Casa de Rui at 1:45 sharp. Traffic permitting; I would be waiting on the sidewalk. Okay. This meant dressing up a bit more than usual for the Casa work, a nice dress shirt, slacks, leather shoes, along with my briefcase.

I arrived at the Casa at 9:00 sharp (it opened at 8:00, an unheard-of hour in Rio). Sebastião was across the research table which turned out to be a good thing. He could fill me in with the "real" scene that would match the "folhetos." I told him it would be just the one session and me leaving at 1:30 to see a friend, so we hustled to get three or four important story – poems from the library for my perusal. The idea was to follow chronologically the important stories since AI – 5's ending in late 1978. The topic for the day would be the "anistia" or national political amnesty approved at the beginning of General Figueiredo's regime.

Geisel ended AI – 5 in 1978, but it would be Figueiredo who would allow political amnesty. He would promise a gradual return to Democracy with a lessening of the censorship imposed in 1964, reaching a high point in 1968 (which

I already witnessed and wrote about in an earlier version of "Letters"). In addition, there would be the promise of free elections for local posts, then state and finally federal. Most everyone could see the writing on the wall; the military sensed the lack of support and the unhappiness of the populace with their strict regime.

The first significant step was the Amnesty Law approved by Congress on August 28, 1979. It permitted the return to public life of many politicians whose rights had been revoked ("cassados") by the Military Regime since AI – 1 in 1964. In reality, two punishments were revoked: the right to serve in political office and the suspension of political rights, that is, the right to vote and to participate in party politics. (This was what Jaime Ferreira had spoken of in our dinner just days before.) The only exception would be for those accused of terrorist acts or armed resistance to the Regime. Little did he know, but Figueiredo in effect opened the floodgates to the protest movement that would culminate in Dante de Oliveira.

In Rio the "political" poet Paulo Teixeira de Sousa wrote "Cordel pela Anistia Completa, Geral e Irrestrita" ["'Cordel' for Complete, General and Unrestricted Amnesty"]. He dared to say that the wrong people were in prison – the politicians who wanted to better Brazil- while the trash of society, drug traffickers and thieves were left to roam the streets. In a nation where only "futebol" was important or allowed and "slogans" like "Brasil – Ame -o ou Deixe -o" ["Brazil – Love It or Leave It"] were spouted, the poet accused the regime:

… O vício e a corrupção/	The vice and corruption
Infestando nossa gente	Infesting our people
É esse "O Brasil p'ra frente"	It's that "Onward Brazil"
Como diz a tradição." p. 3.	As the story is told. p. 3.

The poet appeals to the authorities to not arrest him, for his "only sport is to battle for amnesty. He details only one major case, that of Luís Carlos Prestes, "O Cavaleiro da Esperança" ["The Knight of Hope"]. His message comes from the "povão" ["common man"]: thievery in the government and especially in commerce, has been transformed into the national "pastime" ("futebol" supposedly). The supermarkets rob the poor and the government agencies (Sunab) meant to protect the poor instead of prosecuting the "sharks of commerce" sell out to them.

The popularity of the Law benefited General Figueiredo; there was euphoria throughout the nation. Amnesty was proof of the much-trumpeted political opening! José Soares in Recife waxed euphoric praising the freedom of former leftist governor of Pernambuco, Miguel Arraes. The latter was a favorite and cohort of President João Goulart in the ill-fated campaign for agrarian reform in 1961 to 1963, one of the major causes of the military takeover in 1964.

I used the word "floodgate" for a reason; the political opposition was not content with the abrogation of AI – 5 and the Amnesty Law; they wanted an accounting of the years of violence and the reported 197 Brazilians killed by the military since 1964. That general atmosphere brought an even stronger text by the same "cordel" poet Teixeira: "Os Ex – Exilados e os Desaparecidos" ["The Former Exiles and the Disappeared"]. He begins with an appeal to the Muse not for poetic inspiration, but rather for her protection as he writes his verse. He praises the amnesty of national figures like José Dirceu, Leonel Brizola, Miguel Arraes, and "Companheiro Prestes," calling them "quatro cabras da peste" ["tough SOBS'S"] who never gave up, but added,

… Pior os martirizados	Que estão desaparecidos
Covardemente abatidos	Por perversos homicidas
Que ceifaram suas vidas	Mas também estão perdidos. (p. 3)

… Worse were those martyred	Those that are disappeared
Cowardly beaten down	By perverse murderers
Who snuffed out their lives	But who are also lost. (p. 3)

Teixeira is evidently what we call a "political" or "politicized" poet, not a mainstay in "cordel," but perhaps like Rafael de Carvalho of São Paulo, a voice of the moment. Rodolfo Coelho Cavalcante, on the other hand a true "professional" of "cordel," abandons his years of support of the Military daring to say,

Fazei com que o presidente	Assuma os 10.000 crimes
Deste tão rude regime …	Conhecido por Fascismo
Que põe o Brasil no abismo	E que tanto nos oprime. (p. 7)

Make the president	Take responsibility for the 10,000 crimes
Of this cruel regime	Known as Fascism
Que takes Brazil to the abyss	And which oppresses us so much. (p. 7)

For Rodolfo, the voice of Anti – Communism and support for the Revolution of 1964 to say these words shows how much the atmosphere in Brazil had changed since April 1 of the latter year.

21st of November 1979: one final example shows the changing times: Abraão Batista of Juazeiro do Norte's diatribe "Debate da ARENA com o MDB em Praça Pública Antes de Morrer" ["The Debate between ARENA and MDB in the Public Plaza Before Dying"]. I paraphrase: "MDB said it this way: O' Arena you are so cruel; you killed students, from shoeshine boys to college graduates. You tortured the innocent; you have the soul of a serpent; St. Isabel help me!" Arena responded very proudly: "Shut the hell up you brute of an animal, or you will end up in hot water! AI – 5 is gone, but our sword is not, something you never respected!

Enough said, this smattering of "cordel" documents that year of appeal for the institution of Amnesty, but the danger in Brazil is not over, the times are particularly tense now four years later with presidential indirect elections coming up next year in the national congress. And the military is leaving no doubt it is still in charge and with lethal means to back its policies. That is what would lead me to the conversation with Maria Aparecida later that afternoon.

17

The Rio Centro Affair – An Unexpected Source

Maria Aparecida did indeed pick me up as planned right in front of the Casa de Rui in a very snazzy new VW Blue Sedan (with all the trimmings). São Clemente was busy, but she pulled into a bus stop, honked once, and I hurried over and jumped in. And off we zoomed; that is the word for it since she was a fast but careful driver, and she said "lunch" would be at a surprise place, a fine Italian restaurant in the back of Leblon near the Lago Rodrigo de Freitas. She was dressed in, uh, "stylish casual" in black form fitting slacks, a blue sweater which enhanced just another of her many charms, low cut enough to just suggest but not overwhelm. Not that I would notice, right? I did notice the small gold cross and chain. She put a warm right hand on my left thigh, and it was "off to the races." She laughed, saying,

> "O' Arretado, é bom saber que ainda tem tudo em ordem, que tesão! Se ve que você precisa de uma boa foda, meu bem. Talvez posso encaminhar tudo depois do almoço."

> "Oh, Arretado, it is good to see that everything is working, what an erection!

> It is clear you need a good 'screw,' my love. Perhaps I can facilitate that after lunch."

69

I said, "You're right about that, but I'm off limits remember? We're here to have a good time at lunch and maybe you help me fill in some blanks on events in Brazil. That does not mean I do not appreciate your suggestion."

"You can't blame a girl for trying, but hey, maybe you'll change your mind. If I'm not wrong, you might remember we did pretty well in 'filling in blanks" back at the Castelo a few years ago." And she laughed again.

We wheeled into a very busy back street of Leblon with a "Trattoria Roma" sign in front; she double parked the car, said "Oi" ["Hi"] to the young valet who came out immediately, and motioned me to get out. "You senhor Gaherty are my escort for the afternoon, and I'm used to first class company, can you handle it?"

I think I turned red, nodded yes, and took her hand and we were ushered into a beautiful patio with a view to the lake by the maître' addressing her as "Senhora Vieira," and saying,

> "O prazer é nosso, que bom ver-te de novo na Trattoria. Imagino que tudo vai bem em São Paulo!" ["The pleasure is ours, how good to see you once again at the Trattoria. I imagine everything is going well in São Paulo!"]

After seating us at a quiet table, there was a flurry of movement by what seemed a squad of waiters, ice water in fine crystal glasses, and a bottle of champagne and equally fine fluted glasses. Maria Aparecida said she did not think I would mind some bubbly even though it was early afternoon and said the demitasse café later would perk me up. I don't remember, who is counting, but I think our glasses were filled three times before the "primero piatto," then the pasta and our main course would arrive.

"I've been looking forward so much to this Miguel; it is an opportunity you to see perhaps the 'girl,' or should I now say 'lady' I have always wanted to be, alone with a magnificently handsome North American who respects me, and we can even talk of high culture!"

"I'm no less pleased and if this is the way you lead your 'other life,' then I'm glad to be a part of it. You know, 'Maria Aparecida' seems so long, what shall I call you? Maria? Aparecida?"

"Maria is best for now. So what have you been doing to fill time in Rio, I mean aside from the 'folhetos de cordel' at that dusty old library at the Casa? I know you have had some catching up to do in town." She smiled. Uh, how much to say? I told her about the meeting with Cláudia up at the Othon and Sofia's scene. She laughed, "Too much to handle in one day, hein? I know about that Sofia Rodrigues woman through a near customer, or, I should say a close business acquaintance, her husband of the moment!"

"Nossa! Maria, you weren't kidding about knowing folks in town, were you? I may need your advice about that; she insisted on a meeting back up at the Othon this coming Saturday and I am still not sure what to do about it."

"Miguel, I can't help unless I know more. How did you ever meet her and get involved with that Black Widow?"

I thought a moment and decided to spill the whole story, that is, the short version without all the details on the hot sex of those encounters a few years ago. Maria could well enough fill in all those blanks. Her response, "Porra! Arretado! No wonder you didn't have time to see me at the Castelo more often! I guess I shouldn't be surprised, you are indeed a 'prize.' But Sônia Rodrigues is indeed a good imitation of a Black Widow, and she gets what she wants. But like those lady spiders, I think she devours her partners after the fun is over. If you really get in a tight spot, you can mention you know her husband is a good customer of mine. Wait! No! That's not a good idea." She thought for a while and said, "You aren't going to like this, but your 'Ace in the Hole,' pardon the crude reference, is that you have been treated for a very serious venereal disease. Pardon me, but with your past escapades here in Rio she will believe that. You don't have to mention specifics, but that the disease is chronic, and treatment is on – going. I think she'll drop you like a hot potato!"

"Nossa! How did we get into this conversation? Table it for now Miguel, and let's enjoy a bit of Italy and Rome right here in Rio! Do you like fried calamari? It's the best in town. The prosciutto and bruschetta the same. I agreed, and when the food came, we also switched to a nice Chianti. It was then when I asked her about Rio Centro, the one big event that the "folhetos" had not touched upon.

She said, "I intentionally asked for a very private table, but just the same, speak lowly. Such matters are still sensitive here. Tell me what you know, then perhaps I can fill in some blanks and give you my perspective."

"Maria, here's a synopsis. "Cordel" the last few days has not revealed anything. It's as though it didn't happen. But conversations with my friends the Ferreiras and even Heitor Dias have given me at least a sketchy idea. I'm aware that General Geisel's role in starting 'abertura' was prime: avoiding the hard – liners, getting General Figueiredo to succeed him and most of all ending AI – 5. The dam broke with all the subsequent freedom to report, write, and broadcast without the censorship. The political 'criminals' were allowed to come home, speeches were given, street manifestations returned, and mainly the MDB made significant gains in local and regional politics. The climate was definitely leading to political change and perhaps an end to the dictatorship.

"I'm also privy to information that the military hard -liners, cut out of much of the action by 'abertura' and local elections, never gave up and were convinced to keep the military in power. They did it with phony 'bombings by leftists' and threats to officials even in the Catholic hierarchy who had supported 'abertura,' but some thought that Rio Centro would be the biggest effort to reverse democratization. The central figure was Army Colonel and Commander of the Rio de Janeiro Police Force, Newton Cerqueira. Right, so far?"

"More than you can imagine. I'll just fill you in on the event: Rio Centro convention center holds 20,000 people and on April 30th there was to be a big "espetáculo" concert to celebrate "Day of the Workers," May 1st the next day. Almost all the entertainers including Alcéu Valença, Gal Costa, Beth Carvalho and your good friend Chico Buarque were set to perform. What happened was a fiasco, a scene of utter chaos and confusion, and as most of us suspect, downright incompetence by the police. A secret police campaign was set up to have graffiti covering all the Rio Centro Billboards with the initials of the VPR, 'Vanguarda Popular Revolucionária' ['Popular Revolutionary Vanguard'], a leftist group not heard from since 1973. Several bombs went off nearby, one in a power station which was to cut all power to the performance venue, and another in an unmarked car with 'unauthorized off – duty police officers' in the Rio Centro parking lot, all in an effort to blame the Left for the threat of bombs and possible deaths in the auditorium. In effect the operation was bungled – the bombs exploded at the venue, but panic ensued, and people came to check on family and friends at the concert, and there was a huge traffic jam. The military government covered it all up, the whole bloody plan, and no 'stain' was placed on President Figueiredo.

"Now, Miguel, perhaps you can put two and two together. It was a military and Rio de Janeiro police plan to prove the Left had not been vanquished in Brazil and were still a threat to national security. It turned out to be the last 'hurrah' from them, and the reverberation of the act and other events to come led us to where we are today, on the cusp of a return to Democracy.

"The fly in the ointment, Miguel, is your friend and mine, Heitor. He has never said a word to me, and I don't dare ask, but later that night he showed up at the Castelo, and he was shaken. He drank a lot more than usual, spent time with one of his favorite girls, and didn't leave until early on May Day."

"Maria, it's just three years later, and Heitor told me of his promotion to Captain and that he now in fact oversees the entire South Zone police in Rio. I've never doubted his commitment and faith in the regime. He would do whatever necessary to support it and in fact has hinted to me that their time is not over."

"Miguel, that's what we know, that's all I know, and I sincerely ask you to not take the matter further. If you must write about it, do so in very general detail *after* you get back home and be sure to mention it only in connection to the lack of reporting in 'cordel.' Heitor is a good friend, a long – time friend, a good customer and I intend to keep it that way. You must know, there is no link, zero, nada, absolutely nothing linking him personally to Rio Centro. And, Miguel, "em boca fechada, não entram moscas" ["loose lips sink ships"].

We poured another glass of Chianti and Maria suggested the veal parmigiana with Italian salad. There was small talk, she speaking of her two lives, more details on the condo in the Barra and once again her dream of retirement and travel, laughing, "maybe to a real trattoria in Roma!"

I accepted the Italian demitasse café and even a refill. Maria looked across the table at me and repeated a saying of the times, "E, agora, José?" She slipped her hand on my thigh under the table. "I'll give you a minute to think it over."

"Christ! You the reader cannot imagine how those three words tortured me! Brazilians had called me "bobo" ["dummy"] or even "seu burro" ["you idiot"] when I tried to explain that some of us Catholics were different, that marriage meant something. Even though I had evolved to a progressive and a bit of a "cherry picker Catholic," that inherited morality was still with me. I joked that at least I had not contacted the "clap" again like in bachelor days up in Recife, or worse! There would be zero chance of venereal disease with this lady. And no one, absolutely no one, would every tell Molly. Except me, the guilty, cradle Catholic raised to never lie, and frankly, unable to do so.

Maria said, "I think I anticipated how all this would turn out, and you know, its okay, not all okay, but okay. You can repay me, and I don't mean in any financial or social way, with just being my friend. I have not forgotten your words of encouragement a few years ago. And whenever you want to talk about Brazilian Literature and even debate some minor points, I'm your girl."

I leaned over, planted a quick kiss on those warm lips, and said, "Take me home or at least to the nearest bus stop. This has been a memorable day in my life, and I promise to see you again before I leave."

18

CHICO, "PASSAREDO," AND THE VISTA CHINESA

Next day was Thursday the 25th and my "compromisso" ["appointment"] with Chico Buarque to repeat our hike up to the "Vista Chinesa" and see all the wildlife and birds along the way. I knew the drill from what was it? 1969. Seemed so long ago and a different era, at least politically. And I would do a lot more huffing and puffing, now 14 years later. I wore walking shorts, a t – shirt with a pocket for a small notepad and ink pen to write down bird names, tennis shoes and a baseball style sun hat. Chico the same but with no hat. We both had small water bottles we could latch onto our belts. The final item was a small pair of binoculars and a small bird book Chico had in a small pouch but asked me to carry. Okay.

Not much had changed; we walked through the back of the Jardim Botânico and then started a steep climb on a well – worn trail and soon into deep woods. Chico walked fast but seemed fine with my requests for rest stops and that's when we talked. I haven't mentioned it, but Pope John Paul II did a big trip to Brazil in 1980, and "cordel" went nuts with a plethora of stories by poets all over the Northeast and down to Rio and São Paulo. It was one of the few "safe" topics in the time of Censorship. Chico had a very conservative upbringing in Catholic schools and circles as a teenager, but like me and many others, was now irregular at Mass and critical of church affairs. But he did give the Archbishop in São Paulo full credit for standing up to the military and of course was a big admirer of "The Red Bishop" Dom Hêlder Câmara up in Recife. I repeat just one comment on that: the archbishop was labeled a "commie" way back in the 1960s for his stance on

Liberation Theology, and defense and "preference for the poor." His worst sin was his mantra of those times: "The worst violence is hunger.'"

On another stop Chico burst out laughing and I thought he would never stop. "Did you hear about the Jules Rimet Trophy? Like we say, "Só no Brasil" ["Only in Brasil!"]. I had heard of it. It turns out "cordel" had a scathing story - poem by iconoclast poet Franklin Maxado in São Paulo. *The* gold and silver trophy for winning the World Cup three times had given Brazil the right to keep it, temporary ownership, and the damned thing was stolen from a glass show window in downtown Rio in 1983. There could be no greater dishonor and embarrassment to Brazil. The thing was recovered but the damage had been done, i.e. don't trust the Brazilians with anything! Chico said, "The generals should have just had me guard it out at my amateur 'futebol' stadium of Politeama in the Barra. We all would have been better off!"

We talked about "Passaredo," Chico and Francis Hime's ode to the birds of Brazil, ecology and an effort to save them. "That tune was in the works since 1975, but with the beginning of the ecological movement around the world, Philips finally went along with me adding it to an album just recently. But the 'genesis' was this walk, or rather, a couple of hundred of these walks over the years. Porra, Miguel! It's no mystery what happens to nature when the Military pushed massive economic development in the Amazon the last fifteen years! You want to know about it: how about "pintassilgo, pintaroxo, melro, uirapiru, asa branca" and a hundred more! I'll get you the tape when we get back home."

The binocs and bird book paid off. We saw two varieties of brilliantly colored Toucans, all kinds of other tiny birds with names in Portuguese, checked out in the bird book, my favorites always the most brilliantly colored. I wrote a few down in my notepad: Glittering Bellied Emerald, Yellow – Olive Flycatcher, Golden Crowned Warbler, Flame Crested Tanager, Blue Dacnis and others. Chico knew most but checked them all out in the book. A goldmine!

And there were the animals: agoutis, two or three snakes, and several Saguí monkeys. I asked if it was always this way and Chico said, yes and no, we were having a spectacularly lucky day. And not as many as there used to be.

On another rest stop I got back to politics and with Maria Aparecida and Rio Centro still on my mind, asked Chico about the latter. He frowned, and guffawed: "Os macacos!" ["The apes!]. Brazilians' derogatory term for the "fuzz" or cops. He affirmed the business, now known by most Brazilians, of the leadership by the Rio Head of Police, but said,

"O'! Tudo saiu pela culatra e estimulou bastante a onda da democratização que vivemos hoje! Viva Comandante Cerqueira!" ["It all backfired and brought on much of the democratization we have today! Long live Commander Cerqueira!"]

"We, the entertainers were all set to go on stage when the whole place erupted, noise, smoke, chaos and rampant, contradictory shouts of what was going on. We only learned later, like most Brazilians, of the bomb at the power station and the farce of the bombs going off in the police car. Good riddance I say."

The rest of the hike was uneventful, at least compared to last time. There were no DOPS people up on top checking on Chico, just dozens of tourists looking at the spectacular view. We tarried just a bit and Chico said, "Bora! Muito a fazer lá embaixo esta tarde." ["Let's go, lots to do down there below this afternoon."] His clip down was faster even than on the way up, you had to be careful where you placed your feet, and we soon arrived back at the house. He said, "You'll stay for almoço of course, hein, Arretado? I want to play the "Passaredo" tape for you plus another I think you will find very interesting; it will hit the streets before next week's concert. And maybe we can rehearse your bit part in the concert next week." No argument on my part about all that.

After a great Brazilian "almoço" of all my favorite foods (the family knew by now what I would eat or maybe turn up my nose at with a perfunctory "my stomach can't handle that, sorry"), Chico played the "Passaredo," and I had to hear it maybe four times to even begin to get all the birds' names. Chico 'fessed up he had not seen nearly all of them but could vouch for their existence from his well - worn bird manual. "Arretado, o que precisei mais foi a rima." ["Arretadado, what I really needed was the rhyme."] And he laughed. But the point of the song was well made: "O homem vem aí" ["The man is coming over there"] and a dire warning to birdkind! "I'm not an ornithologist but have friends who are, and they say it is all coming to pass. Most people don't know that there were more birds in the Atlantic Rain Forest than the Amazon, and there's only about 5 per cent of it left in Brazil, and we saw a bit of it this morning."

After a couple of "doses de cachaça" [shots of 'cachça] and more beer for me, Chico got really excited, and said, "I want you to hear this. It will hit the streets tomorrow." It was "Pelas Tabelas," a great tune with percussion and background like that of a real Carnival samba parade. As usual, it was the lyrics that gave it the "Chico Buarque" label. Here's a sample:

> Ando com minha cabeça já pelas tabelas
> Claro que ninguém se toca com minha aflição
> Quando vi todo mundo na rua de blusa amarela
> Eu achei que era ela puxando um cordão. …

> I'm walking with my head down in the dumps
> No one can feel my affliction for sure
> When I saw everyone in the streets with yellow shirts
> I realized it was a Carnival group passing by.

The "he" in the song dances in the streets and hears the entire city beating on the pots and pans. He sees the people coming down from the "favelas" and thinks they are asking for the head of the man looking at the favelas, the head later rolling in Maracanã soccer stadium and later on a tray.

He said, "Escuta a música e vê se você percebe o miolo! Ra ra." ["Listen to the song and see if you get the gist! Ha ha."] I listened three times, admitted it made me want to dance samba (gringos can't dance samba) and go back to Carnival and "Orféu Negro." But also that much of it I couldn't make out, at least not at first: "Who exactly is 'ela?' The people descending from the 'favelas' dressed in yellow and blue, beating on the pans for percussion, dancing in the streets. That seems simple enough, again like 'Orféu Negro,' and the dancing. But the 'cabeça rolando in the Maracanã,' nossa, that is too much. Wait! There's a wild possibility. Is it President Figueiredo busy with his government files and hearing the ruckus and noise and music outside and begins to wonder? Why not? There will be at least one hundred interpretations."

Chico retorquiu:

"Eu te dou 3 dicas: os comícios de 'Diretas já' uns poucos meses atrás, a volta da Democracia, e um presidente. ["I'll give you three hints: the manifestations of 'Direct Elections' a few months ago, the return of Democracy and a President"]. The song is intensely happy and reflects the euphoria of those huge 'comícios" ['political protest parades'] in Rio and São Paulo just a few months before the Dante de Oliveira vote. You figure out the rest. Spend some of those yânqui dollars tomorrow and get the cassette, and we'll have another conversation in a week or two, tá?"

I would have the sound and lyrics of the song ringing in my head for the next two weeks!

The day was wearing on and we decided we had had enough "farra" [partying] for the moment. Chico reminded me of the rehearsal next Friday at the Maracanazinho for the concert, said to practice "Manhã de Carnaval" and the rock tunes. If I got to his house at 10:00 that morning I could ride along in the van with the band. "Topo. Até lá. And thanks for the hike and the day, another memorable time."

The highlight of that evening was a long call to Molly assuring her I was fine, research continuing to go well at the Casa de Rui, the great hike with Chico, the birds, and the concert to come in a week. No mention of Brazilian women, and she didn't ask. There was nothing scandalous to say anyway. I wanted to know all about Claire, now walking, talking, getting into everything. And time to exchange some private small talk of old lovers.

Flávio had loaned me one of his guitars before going to Buenos Aires, so I spent three hours late into that night going over the old Rock n' Roll and especially "Manhã de Carnaval." It sounded just okay, and I hoped it would be a whole lot better with the band next week. I'm thinking, "Seu burro! ["You idiot!"]. How did you get yourself into this?" But then I remembered the concerts and the fun back in '71. Can you go back "home" again?

One cause for little sleep that night was I got to thinking about the "date" with Sônia at the Othon coming up Saturday night. I remembered Maria Aparecida's advice and the "ace in the hole." Hmm. Tomorrow I'll get back to the Casa and do yet another reading on the "folhetos." Sebastião says there are some good stories yet to come.

19

CLOSER TO THE FINISH LINE WITH "CORDEL" AND 1984

Friday, June 26th, still keeping busy but on track for the scheduled weeks in Brazil. Up early, fruit, "pão e manteiga e café com leite" brought down by Marcela, courteous as always. It's a "work" day so it's briefcase, jeans, tennis shoes, t – shirt and an umbrella and off I go to Princesa Isabel and the short hop on the subway to São Clemente in Botafogo. I know I've said it before, but I like that twenty-minute walk up to the Iron Gate and entrance to the Casa de Rui, the walk through the garden with all the big ferns and shade trees and then to the concrete and glass research center, second floor and the "Cordel" Section.

Only Sebastião was in the room, but he greeted me warmly, asked for cafezinhos from the kitchen and seemed prepared to hear my news since last I saw him. Since he was not privy to my dealings with Maria Aparecida, no need to talk of that, but I did tell him of being back with Chico Buarque and our hike and bird walk up to Vista Chinesa. Sebastião, like so many Brazilians and "cariocas," keeps songbirds in cages in the open patio next to his kitchen at the apartment in Glória; he talked of the "Rouxinol do Rio Negro" as his favorite.

I remarked the summer was moving on, research okay, no need to go up to São Cristóvão yet, but wondered what else he might have to keep me entertained in Rio. That was when I got the surprise. I had seen a reference to "Umbanda" in one of the "folhetos" on politics, and knowing it was big in Rio, asked Sebastião about it, figuring he would have the standoffish attitude most middle and upper class educated "cariocas" would have about it. Ao contrário! [To the contrary!] We talked of how the poets of "cordel" almost always spoke disparagingly of it, always defending Catholicism against such things.

Sebastião said, "True, true, but their attitude is largely an uninformed and even ignorant and biased view. Umbanda is like any other religion, has its own tenets and practices, and we Brazilians especially are supposed to, ha, respect all ethnicities and their beliefs. I think the 'cordel' poets associate it mainly, and mistakenly, with African religion and the black race in Brazil. You *have* noticed their prejudice on race, right? It goes way back in the Northeast, and I think may be associated, at least somewhat, to post – slavery days in 1888 when the poor, white 'lavradores' [rural farm laborers] all of a sudden had to complete with 'pretos' [blacks] and their labor. And that coincidentally was the time of the advent of the old 'cantadores' [oral improvisers of verse] and just a decade or two later Leandro Gomes de Barros, Francisco das Chagas Batista and 'cordel.' The old 'pelejas' [poetic duels] have blackness and prejudice as one of the main themes, Ignacio da Catingueira the most famous case. And you know the terms 'negro, nego, negrada' in 'cordel' may even be associated with the devil and hell. And the term 'moleque' [poor, black boy] is always used for the devil's helpers in hell."

"Sebastião, how does this relate to the uproar of Ariano Suassuna making Jesus a black man in the 'Auto da Compadecida?'"

"Hey, Miguel, I don't know, but he says it is a reaction to North American racism. You tell me."

"Well, that's bullshit for sure. A big subject for now. You know as well as I do that any black person in Brazil falls over laughing (if the conversation is with a serious researcher) when you talk of Brazil's 'racial democracy,' and especially in the Northeast when they read of the 'great' Gilberto Freyre talking of the 'beleza' of those 'mucambos' [slums] near the ocean south of Recife. Yeah, I've seen and noticed all those racial references in the 'cordel,' especially 'negrada.'"

"Anyway Miguel, I would estimate at least 25 per cent of Umbanda followers today are white. That is, in Rio. You might as well know, I am a believer and practitioner."

"I'm surprised and I guess shocked, although it does not make me think any the less of you, just that there is another side to you."

"Miguel, the best way to explain all this is to show it to you. How about being my guest next Tuesday at a Session close by here in Flamengo; it's the main 'terreiro' [place of worship] I attend, mainly because it is close to home in Glória and its atmosphere suits me. I think in all honesty you as a scholar, researcher and more importantly, a university professor specializing in Brazil, need to know about this and have an accurate opinion."

"You've got me there, old friend, can't argue with that. And I'm curious, so you are on for next Tuesday. Can we table it now? I've got three or four important 'cordel' poems to get through today. Maybe we can talk more at lunch."

"That depends on who is with us. I do not advertise my affiliation and am willing to talk about it, but there are many folks here at the Casa that do not think the same and maybe would not understand. So let's not get into that at lunch, okay?"

"Nossa, I don't know if I can get this out of my head right now, but I'll give it a try. I had a small stack of story – poems on the table and began to peruse them. What a hoot! They were great, and like so many times before, if I had language questions or equally important, plain questions on how they reflected the times, my encyclopedic friend was just across the table.

First is "O Pacote" ["The Economic Package"] by Azulão, reflecting an attitude I would soon learn of the economic and political reality of the "povo" accompanying all the politics since 1979 – anger and frustration from the economic crisis which would heat up the political cauldron for the next five years. The main theme: the economy under the Military turned out worse for the poor, most Brazilians, and especially under the leadership of finance minister Delfim Neto. Azulão's is a scathing commentary on the "Pacote" by the FMI [The International Monetary Fund] which demanded economic reform and an austerity budget to try to straighten out Brazil, to raise cash to pay off the horrendous international debt owed by Brazil. The poet is furious,

Inventaram esse pacote	They invented that "package"
Para embrulhar a nação	To hoodwink the Nation
Mas nele só tem aperto	But in it there is only belt – tightening
Carestia e inflação	A higher cost of living and inflation …

The poet has some good questions: Whatever happened to all the gold mined in Carajás and Serra Pelada that was supposed to back the "cruzeiro"? And where is all the oil that Petrobrás claims to have found? And why is it the more oil is supposedly found in Brazil, the more expensive are its derivatives like gasoline? Brazil needs a man who will fight the rampant political corruption, the "ghost" jobs given to politicians' families and the bureaucrats. But worst of all is all the above caused by Delfim Neto and the huge foreign debt and economic crisis.

Another of my favorite "cordel" poets with "cojones" to tell it like it is (albeit, after AI – 5) is Gonçalo Ferreira de Silvia, and he joins Azulão with "Delfim Deu Fim ao Brasil" ["Delfim Did In Brazil"] in a clever play – on – words in the title. In short, he says Delfim and the government have lied to the people for years and the proof: the more starvation attacks the Brazilians, the fatter Delfim gets! (He was notoriously overweight as the years went by).

To show he has no fear in these post censorship days, Gonçalo goes on to criticize the sacred cow, the President himself, in "Presidente João Teimoso" ["President John the Stubborn"]. In a scathing attack the poet laments the President's travel junkets and most of all, the now "pharaonic projects" of the Military: the Trans Amazon Highway, the Rio – Niterói Bridge, the Itaipu Dam and Hydroelectric Project, and yes, the subway in Rio (all familiar to my readers from "Letters II and III"), all built with "funny money" which created that incredible international debt. He advises the President to not hesitate in resigning, since he (the "pres") already admitted publicly he had neither the vocation nor the will to have the job!

Azulão repeated the same theme but in great language in "Brasil Chorando" ["Brazil Crying"] saying,

Depois que o homem fez	After *the man* made
Cavalo da Nação	A horse out of the nation
Botou a sela e montou -se	He put on the saddle and mounted up
Soltou as rédeas da mão	And gave it free rein …

The result was the economic disaster already described. There was a bandied about rumor in Brazil that General Figueiredo who was originally a cavalry general knew a lot more about horses and liked them better than people.

These were the story – poems that I came back to Brazil hoping to find! They led to the "Diretas Já" campaign which was what I had left to see in the next few days in Brazil.

20

SÔNIA RODRIGUES AND MY NERVES

Saturday came and I admit to frazzled nerves, thinking of Sônia that night. I cleaned up and took the Jardineira Bus along Avenida Atlântica to the Othon, going up to the top floor and the bar at 7:00 p.m. Not knowing what was to come, I figured I better stick to beer at least until Sônia would come. And she did, making a quiet entrance from the elevator over to my table, smiling, and even asking if she could sit down. "Claro que sim."

I had learned by now, you never know, a smile and a kiss or an angry accusation; fortunately, at least this time it was the former. She bent over, pecked me on the cheek and said, 'Tréguas Miguel, … por enquanto. Obrigada por chegar" ["Peace, Michael, … for now. Thank you for coming"]. I answered carefully, saying, "We would not have wanted things to end like our last meeting here, right?"

Sônia was indeed an eyeful as usual, a tight blue top showing off her assets, a short skirt just above the knees, hair and makeup like she just came from the beauty parlor, which is probably did. (An aside from Rio: if one walks by a beauty salon anytime on Saturday afternoon or very early evening, many are open to the street, and you see all the women getting dolled up for Saturday night.) She called for the waiter, not conferring with me, and ordered a Chivas double on the rocks, supposedly for me, and a half bottle and flute of champagne for herself. "I remember you like this foreign stuff and can't afford the tariffs in Brazil, but you may remember that it's no problem for me. Is that all right?"

We looked at each other for a moment, both waiting for the other to begin, than both of us starting at the same time and then laughing. Good medicine under the circumstances, but I said, "I think you first, Sônia." Here is the beginning of that conversation:

"Miguel, you are as handsome as ever, a little less hair on top, a bit heavier around the waist, but the same guy, I think. We certainly had our times that summer of 1969, didn't we? Here in the Othon Suite, out in the condo and on the beach in the Barra and our last night here again. No need to get embroiled in all that right now. I've done a lot of thinking since a week ago when I lost it up here with you and Cláudia; I apologize. But Mike, let me give you my take on all this and how it has turned out, and I promise, no histrionics, tá? ["Ok?"]

She didn't wait for my answer. "I thought we really clicked, that it was a great match. I remember telling you what amounts to my 'life story' of love, romances, breakups and all the rest. And what I and the Rodrigues family could do for you and me if you just said yes. But I do remember your answer, heartfelt I think, that the Nebraska farm boy could never adapt to such a life in Rio. And I couldn't leave my family and all the business opportunities it offered here. We talked tentatively of a meeting that Fall in San Francisco with what I hoped would be a romantic rendezvous and maybe a change of mind on your part. That was when that one telephone conversation ended my dream. I remember saying that I would fly to San Francisco in a moment to meet you, porra, I would fly to the moon for you. Am I right up to now?"

"Yes, but that was when I told you of a renewal of my relationship with Molly in D.C. and our hopes for the future."

"Miguel, I hung up on you, but that phone call threw me into a tailspin that took three months to recover from. I want you to know about that. I was suffering intense depression, began taking way too many pills to end it, unable to work, and dreaming, or maybe hallucinating that I would talk to Daddy and make the wheels turn to force you to come back to Rio and me. (She began to cry softly and dabbed away the tears with a hanky. I just listened.) I soon realized that was not possible. Since then, so long ago but still like yesterday, by the way isn't it unlucky in your culture, the number 13? Since then, now 13 years have passed and here we are.

"Miguel, I have been married three times, now Rogério Alves the third. No need to go into all that, but we have two beautiful children whom we both adore, but he like most Brazilian men, is unfaithful and has his 'nights out' with all the excuses. She laughed a short laugh. But you remember Rodrigues Limited and our detectives. Nothing escapes them. So what to do? Rogério is at least a good man, a good father, treats us well, and life goes on. But, …, Miguel, you would have been faithful, I know it, and I still think I could love you again."

"Sônia, can we have a nice dinner, but more private, I think down on the third-floor mezzanine with a private table overlooking the beach. I have nothing but good memories of that from past years. And maybe just enjoy each other's company?"

She shook her head yes and said she would arrange the whole thing. So, we got up, I took her hand and we got in the elevator and headed down to the third floor.

Once settled, she called over the bar man, explained the special arrangement and that we should have our privacy in the corner with glassed in views of the entire beach, that our maître would take care of the dining. Conversation was still pleasant, she wanting to know my news of this stay in Rio (as though she would not probably know already, vis a vis Rodrigues detectives). I told her of the terrific research results from São Cristóvão and the Casa de Rui, great comradeship with former student Flávio and the latest with Chico Buarque. And, uh, of the upcoming concert next Saturday at the Maracanazinho and "reunion" of "Mistakes of Our Youth" and maybe with an extra song or two and all the practice I needed to put in between now and then.

Sônia laughed and was genuinely excited, "I'll get tickets for that with my girlfriends, girls' night out maybe, no need for husbands around. Maybe I can toss my bra and panties up on stage when you are on! Don't worry, I'll have an extra set in my purse, no need to embarrass you." The waiter came and Sônia ordered for both of us, saying she knew my favorites so no guesswork there. We both had champagne and maybe got a little buzzed; it was congenial, and it was fun. No denying. Filet mignon, lobster, rice pilaf, veggie salad, no dessert, but wonderful cafezinhos."

"Do you still smoke in Rio and toss the pack in the 'basura' ['waste can'] at the Galeão on the way out of town? I've always admired such discipline."

"No, haven't for a long time, but maybe tonight I could smoke two or three." Sônia called to the waiter, the Marlboros arrived in a minute and we both lit up after the cafezinho. A bottle of Drambuie appeared, and we toasted each other. That Brazilian cliché of the times running through my head, "E, agora José?" ["So, what now?"]. Sônia wanted to know about Georgetown, Molly and Claire, so I filled her in. She was pensive, taking it all in to be sure, and I thought maybe turned a bit wistful.

"Miguel because I love you and want the best for you, I will restrain all my desires and just wish you the best. But there is one proviso, one promise, if anything happens, God forbid, and you are ever free again, will you call me right away and I'll be on the first plane (the company jet you know) to just hold you, cradle you in my arms, and be there for you."

I sincerely thought just a moment and said yes. I would reflect on that moment later, on the airplane when I would head back home. I found no moral wrong and above all any malice in the answer. For the moment it kept the peace. After one more cordial, we agreed to stay in touch by phone, Sônia repeating she would be dancing in the aisles in the Maracanazinho, stood, gave each other a light kiss and went our separate ways.

Dear reader, I apologize for perhaps not meeting your expectations either with more fireworks or titillating detail, but believe me, it's for the best.

21

HOME ALONE

And reader, you already have surmised, Heitor Dias stopped me along the Copacabana "calçada" [mosaic sidewalk] as I walked pensively all the way back to Leme. He said, "You look like you need a drink. Let's go to my 'ponto' ['hangout'] for a drink or two and catch up on 'Arretado's' adventures in Rio." It was an invitation you could not refuse, so I hopped in the black police sedan, shook hands and off we went. The driver dropped us off in front of the "pé sujo" and said he would be back in an hour and a half to pick us up. Okay.

After settling into a cachaça for Heitor and an icy Brahma for me, Heitor smiled, saying, "Eu não posso acreditar! ["I can't believe it!"]. Arretado, you were with Maria Aparecida for dinner and lots of drinks and now Sônia and you still haven't got laid! What's wrong? Did somebody cut off your dick? Or maybe one of those broads hired a macumba "mãe de santo" [female religious leader] to put a hex on you! Ha ha ha. Seriously, I think you're nuts! Well, one more to go, right? How about the Ferreira chick or should I say respectable married lady? You know we keep track of you, General Goeldi's orders, so don't be offended."

I took a big swig of beer, smiled, and said, "Heitor, velho amigo, all is going according to plan, and so far, so good. Remember I'm a married man with a young daughter at home, a progressive Catholic, and just trying to stay out of trouble."

"Por enquanto. Por enquanto. ["For now. For now.] I'm betting you won't make it another week. Let's see, who else is on the list? If all else fails, Maria Aparecida would clear her very busy schedule anytime for you. What's left, 'bater a bronha,' 'fazer punheta'? ['jack off']. That's for men with no possibilities. And that ain't you!"

"Heitor, I think we have this topic covered, okay? I've got a couple of questions however and you may be able to help me. The 'cordel' reporting is really going well, I've got post AI – 5 and amnesty covered, and stuff right up to 'Diretas Já' which I'll be covering this week. Good stuff for bringing research up to date. But there's a glaring hole in the 'cordel' reporting, and I think it's close to home for you here in Rio. Will you stay calm if we talk about it?"

Heitor suddenly became very serious, perhaps anticipating a difficult conversation. "Miguel, you know me, how I think, my politics and mainly my job. You and I are great friends, but believe me, rapaz, [buddy] it could have been otherwise. Go ahead. Shoot."

I took a deep breath. "Heitor, it's Rio Centro. There's not a single story in the 'cordel.' And those guys write about anything going on in Rio. And it's well after AI – 5 was abrogated. They seemed to have written about everything else."

"Pois, I guess it wasn't really that important then, hein, amigo? The only thing I can tell you is that it was some renegade cops, guys I knew of here in Rio. Not just me, but anyone in law enforcement. But I assure you they have been taken care of if you see what I mean. We could have had a helluva disaster, a bomb blown up in a crowd of 20,000 pop music fans. It was resolved; General Figueiredo had no knowledge of it. Case closed. Tá? Let's change the subject and have another beer." It was not a suggestion; Heitor had his "captain's face" on.

Not being entirely stupid, I took the hint and said, "Oi, there's something else a lot more fun going to happen this next week. Chico Buarque is putting on a concert in the Maracanazinho and has invited me to join one of the sets, a reprise of 'Mistakes of Our Youth.' And I may get a chance to do my one Brazilian favorite, 'Manhã de Carnaval.' I would consider it an honor if you could be there and hear it."

"Miguel, I'm way ahead of you. We keep an eye on all of Chico's gigs, including this one, and I've already assigned men to make sure there are no shenanigans. I'll be somewhere in the audience for sure. And guess who else is interested? Your old friend General Goeldi! Word gets around. He's still chafing about 1971 and Vlado Mirzog and Chico stopping the concerts. But, hey, it's a new world out there; I think in fact he sees your 'reunion' as a good thing for the regime right now."

"Heitor, how did you know *I* was going to be involved and what I've just told you? I thought I was surprising you."

"Miguel, come on, give your local police a little more credit than that. It's not rocket science (hey, have you heard he one about the Portuguese sending a rocket to the sun?)

The joke: After the great success of the U.S. landing men on the moon, the Portuguese decided they could top that — send astronauts to the sun. Everyone said, "You are nuts! You'll burn up!" The Portuguese scientists retorted, "No, no, 'a gente vai de noite' [us folks] will go at night."

"Things are not like when we had AI – 5 and pre – censorship, but entertainers do have to do advertising and print programs, and there's a program note about you. Surprised?"

"Surprised and scared shitless. I thought it would all be kind of spur of the moment. My knees are already knocking. Porra! Why would Chico do this? It's one week from tonight; I better get home and practice. Chico told me he and the band could cover any rough spots, but this is a little too much. How in the hell did I get myself into this?"

"Hey, I think it will be a lot of fun and maybe a really good thing for your love life here in Rio. The concert 'brotinhos' are a lot more forward than they were ten or fifteen years ago. I can get you some of those little blue pills your 'big pharma' people are pushing on the TV ads. Ha ha. Have you seen the one in Italy with the little yellow Fusca and the pill that gets dropped? I fell over laughing. Don't plan on getting much sleep that night. We should make a time now for you to give me a report. How about the Monday after the concert, give you time to recuperate?" He laughed hard this time, a belly laugh. And I was just relieved the Rio Centro conversation seemed to be forgotten for the moment.

"Oh, one more thing. On a more serious note. You might need some protection that night. Hard to tell. On the one hand, if Chico and his folks get back into that anti – military shit and rev up the crowd, we'll turn off the electricity and the mikes and close it down. Then all hell will break loose. But I think he's too smart for that "merda" now; hell, his side seems to be winning. Even my crowd is talking amongst ourselves (all unofficial you see). Porra! Maluf will never beat Tancredo in the "indiretas" coming up in January. And we know the concert may turn into another political rally, but we think it will be a happy crowd. We just don't want any surprises, including loose cannons from the old Right."

I ordered another round of drinks, we dug into the snacks, peanuts and the like, and asked Heitor, "Ainda amigos?" ["Still friends?"] I had to ask those questions tonight."

Heitor smiled, patted me on the shoulder and said, "We've been through too much, and more importantly, we know each other well and what's in our heads and hearts. Arretado, you'll never have to worry about me. I'm thinking maybe you could set up a 'learning or research junket' for me to D.C. Maybe even see J. Edgar in the FBI. Ha ha. I won't hold you to that, well, anyway, not now. I just am worried you are turning into a damned 'veado' ['queer']. Homem, you've got to live a little. Life is too short. You're in Rio. Shape up, okay?"

"We'll see. We'll see. Hey, can you pour me in the door at the apartment building now? I got to get on that music."

That was what happened, a ride to the apartment at Leme, and me getting out the guitar for two hours before hitting the sack. Stay tuned.

22

SUNDAY A.M. - A SWIM AT COPACABANA, TO FISHERMAN'S ROCK

I probably did something stupid again Sunday morning, another of Gaherty's mistakes in Brazil. I figured I really needed the exercise, so I donned swim shorts, t-shirt, baseball boné, and old tennis shoes and a towel, and headed down to the beach just a five-minute walk from the apartment. Marcela was off (the maids at least get one day a week off in Rio, but that's only because a couple of progressive congressmen introduced and passed the law), so I had "café com leite e pão doce" at the "boteco" ["café"] on the beach. The waves were beautiful in the morning sun, that turquoise – blue, and they were large enough to roll in and curl and then bang into the shore. Gaherty was always a good swimmer, but maybe not that good.

As I was trying to body surf, something done dozens of times over the years in Brazil, I could feel the undertow begin to pull me out into the deeper water. There was that moment of panic, also experienced before, and then the decision to swim angled to the waves, wait for each successive one to push me a little closer to shore, resting in between and hoping I would not be pulled farther out in between waves. Fortunately, it turned out okay, I was able to get to shore, drag myself up on the sand, and one of the Copa lifeguards was there in an instant.

"Oi gringo, se vê que é gringo, quase que quase acabou teus dias aqui em nosso mar. Como está agora?"

"Hey, 'gringo,' you look like a 'gringo,' you almost ended your days here in our ocean. How are you now?"

I muttered that I was exhausted but otherwise okay. He said,

"Régra número um, nunca mas *nunca* entra no mar sozinho sem companheiros acompanhando, mesmo olhando da praia! Dois: não seja bobo, respeite as ondas, e se precisar, não vá longe da praia. Tá? Eu vi tudo e vi que estava recobrando força para voltar à praia, mas, estava pronto para vir com a bóia de salvação. Acontece aqui todos os dias."

"Rule number 1: never but *never* go into the water without friends with you, even watching from the beach. 2: don't be a dummy, respect the waves, but be careful to not swim far from the beach. Ok? I saw everything and that you were able to get it together to get back to the beach, but I was ready to come with the life preserver. This happens every day."

"Obrigado. Sinto muito. Acho que estava demasiado confiante em mim. Pode ficar certo que aprendi a lição."

"Thanks. I'm sorry. I think I was too overconfident. You can be sure I learned my lesson."

Well, Gaherty seu bobo, maybe you didn't. Before I mean. I damned near drowned in Ipanema during my first year in Brazil, exactly the same situation, but it was worse, really worse. Overconfident, that's it. And stupid. I gathered up my stuff, walked back to the apartment, showered, and lay in bed for an hour, still trembling. Only then did I get the energy to go back to the "boteco" on the beach and have a big breakfast of fried eggs, toast, marmalade, orange juice and coffee. Revived, chagrinned, and still kicking myself in the butt.

What to do now? Sunday and me not a "futebol" fan. I wished Flávio were here, but he is still in Buenos Aires. I decided to get back to Fisherman's Rock at the outcropping on Leme and see what conversation I could dredge up with the locals. Quite a crowd being it was Sunday, all men with long heavy rods, huge reels, and big hooks they were baiting with some kind of a small fish and then tossing the bait far out into the waves down below. Evidently there was no prohibition of alcohol because I saw almost every guy had a cooler with bottles of Brahma or cans of Anárctica. And everybody was smoking. I should have felt at home, right, but it took a while. I bought my own bottle of Brahma, a pack of Marlboros and settled into a lawn chair one of the guys offered me. "Você é ianque não é? ["You are an American, right?"] Checking out the local color huh? Either you are a 'veado' 'cause the women are down on the beach, or you must like fishing. And that's all right with me." He interrupted to bait the nasty looking hook again and gave it a huge heave out into the waves. In a minute or two the rod dipped furiously, and he was grinding away at the reel with about a three foot fish with lots of very sharp teeth. I never did get the name of it.

After he slammed its head a few times on the concrete, he tossed it into a large bucket and said, "Let's rest. You buy me a beer and I'll tell you some stories." The stories were not that great, but he was an interesting guy and worth a page or two in "Letters." He was retired, like most of the old men along the walkway, grey headed, his skin deeply brown tanned from so many days in the sun. He had been a "swabby" in the Brazilian Navy, serving on a Coast Guard Cutter all along the north coast of Brazil as far as Manaus in the Amazon. After twenty years he took his retirement and he and his wife, a carioca he had met years earlier, managed to buy a tiny apartment in one of the old apartment buildings several blocks back of the beach. He of course wondered what in the hell I was doing in Brazil and marveled at my Portuguese.

"You must have been CIA, huh? Ha ha. And you speak Portuguese with a slight 'nordestino' accent. Got to be a story there."

I told him I was in Brazil years ago doing research for my doctoral dissertation, on northeastern folklore mainly in Pernambuco and Bahia, and I was collecting "cordel" which he by the way had never heard of. I said it was in the days of General Castelo Branco and Costa e Silva. He said, "Cara, those were *my* days too. You know, we saved Brazil from the @#$$% communists and I'm proud to have been a part of it. There was chaos in Brazil before the military, and I think history is going to repeat itself now. Be careful out there."

Our beers turned into two or three and it was indeed interesting. It all turned out to be déjà vu from the old days in Pernambuco back in the 1960s with the guys from my boarding house. Sílvio, the navy guy's name, proceeded to lecture me on the basics: Brazilian women are the most beautiful in the world ("Sei por sexperiencia," ra ra."); Portuguese is the world's most difficult language, and

Brazil is potentially the richest country in the world with all its resources. And the military's great development projects would soon make that a reality, i.e., Itaipu and the damn and hydroelectric projects on the major rivers of the north the people don't even know about (he meant the Madeira, the Xingu, the Solimões, the Rio Negro, the Tocantins and others). The Trans – Amazonic Highway would open vast areas to logging, cultivation of crops and cattle ranches, more riches for Brazil! And right here in Rio the Rio – Niterói Bridge solving those 'damned traffic jams,' the widening of Avenida Atlântica and even the beach itself, and the Metrô. "A gente vai bem pra' frente daqueles safados em São Paulo" ["Us folks are way ahead of those bastards in São Paulo."].

I was able to get a word in edgewise but had to be careful talking about it. "Sílvio, when I came to Brazil and the Northeast for research (you're right, I guess some of the accent rubbed off), a big topic of conversation was the 'moamba' or smuggling on the North Coast and even smuggling those hot first Mustang automobiles into Brazil to avoid the tariffs."

He patted my arm, cut me off and laughed, "I was right, you had to be CIA. Not everybody today knows about all that. Yeah, my cutter and the Coast Guard were right in the middle of that. I'll say one thing for those 'cafajestes,' they were damned smart! They smuggled in Marlboros by the hundred of cases, Scotch whiskey the same (oh by the way, we could always take our cut, man, did I drink and smoke well in those years), but yeah, the cars were the big deal. We would catch the bastards red handed, in fact, they almost seemed to be waiting to be picked up. We found out about that later. The cars would be off loaded in São Luís or maybe Fortaleza and impounded by the government. But, guess what? There would always be missing an essential part that would render them useless. The one I remember most – carburetors! It turns out the cars had to be auctioned and the same #$^%^##$s would come to the auction, buy the cars at ridiculously low prices, put the carburetors back in and then sell them for huge profits in all the big cities."

"Sílvio, I have this memory of a USIS guy in Bahia, American of course; he was a big man about town with a Mustang convertible. He seemed to be enjoying Brazil."

I then hit a nerve when I asked Sílvio about what all these big projects might do to the Amazon and nature in Brazil and mentioned I had been hearing about Chico Mendes. He took a big swig of beer, looked at me and just said, "That 'sacana' ['bastard'] should get a real job. He's never worked a day in his life. Hey, it's been a pleasure talking to you Miguel, good luck with all that research and 'cordel' shit;

like I say, I've never heard of it. If I don't see you up here for a while, I'll figure you are spending your time looking for all that 'boceta' ['stuff'] on the beach."

So that's what retired Brazilian fishermen talk about! We shook hands and I said I hoped I'd run into him again before I went back home to teach school in a couple of weeks. He said, "It's been a pleasure, fun to talk to a gringo who isn't a 'cafajeste.'"

23

"LITERATURA DE CORDEL" AND "DIRETAS JÁ"

That next Monday I was back at the Casa de Rui hoping to conclude research on the "cordel" and curiously looking forward to Sebastião Batista's offer to find out more about "Umbanda." First things first: the "cordel" reporting on the most recent phase of political happenings in Brazil and very important to bring things up to date: the "Diretas Já" campaign. The reader knows the time frame, late 1983 to April 25, 1984, the huge popular campaign which *Veja* magazine called the most significant popular political campaign in the history of Brazil with street demonstrations culminating in the marches in Rio and São Paulo with one million participants!

From the beginning of the campaign until its end the poets of "cordel" wrote, printed, and sold dozens of titles. They in effect expressed the opinion of the masses, influenced by the national media that saw the end of the military and holding hope that a civilian candidate for president (and his victory) would somehow, some way, ameliorate and solve the political and economic problems facing the nation. The military would allow the campaign, up to a point.

Abraão Batista of Juazeiro do Norte wrote "Encontro dos Presidenciáveis no Largo da Carioca no Rio de Janeiro" ["Encounter of the Presidential Candidates in the Carioca Plaza in Rio de Janeiro"] at the beginning of the campaign which eventually would lead to the contest between the government party [PDS] candidate Paulo Maluf, former governor of São Paulo State, versus Tancredo Neves, longtime politician, national congressman from Minas Gerais and candidate of the people's party the PMDB. And then to the Dante de Oliveira Amendment for direct presidential elections. The peoples' hopes were tied to more of a national political sentiment than practical economics. The amendment was defeated. It brought this "folheto" by Apolônio Alves dos Santos in Rio de Janeiro, representing dozens of other "cordel" texts: "Eleições Diretas Já para um Novo Presidente" ["Direct Presidential Elections for a New President"] May 3, 1984:

Queremos um Presidente …	We want a President …
Dentro do socialism	Within a social movement
Que ofereça vantagem	Who offers hope
Com menos politicagem	With less politiking
Chega de militarsmo!	Enough of Militarism!

Perhaps more to the point in reflecting the national anxiety was a paid "cordel' story poem in Pernambuco by "Friends of Miguel Arraes" – "Nós Queremos Eleições Diretas Agora Para Todos os Brasileiros" ["We Want Direct Presidential Elections Now for All Brazilians"]. They used a fictional author – "Leandro Poeta Popular" sure to attract the attention of the remaining traditional "cordel" public because all would think of the great Leandro Gomes de Barros, famous among other things for his wonderful political satire early in the 20th century. I had done a chapter in the dissertation on the same poet. The story – poem laments the twenty years without political rights in Brazil, the "bionic senators" also called "senadores de proveta" ["test tube senators"] created by the then government party ARENA to guarantee their majority in the national congress. Economics and the national economic depression and crisis were most on their minds: with the successful election Brazil would indeed end the dictatorship and give a big "bananão" ["finger or maybe Italian elbow"] to the international bankers of the IMF responsible for the economic misery throughout the country.

Editorial aside: Brazil had borrowed that old Italian gesture of bending the right arm into a perpendicular motion, slapping the right bicep with the left hand, "dar uma banana" as it were. Okay. "Up yours!"

This is just a sampling of the almost unanimous tone of the dozens of "cordel" story – poems. Alas, Dante de Oliveira failed as already told in our narrative, and all would be left to the Indirect Election coming up next January. I would be back in the U.S. ensconced in the classroom at Georgetown. I, we, could only rely on public sentiment now in July – the massive support for Tancredo Neves and deep dislike of the military's candidate Paulo Maluf.

I finished this and other story – poems excited and satisfied research was now current - and would mail a "Letter" to Hansen of the "Times" with my report and editorial comments. This was after all what they had hired me to do this summer in Brazil.

I had lunch that day with Sebastião and we decided on the "Umbanda" session for the next day in Flamengo, he offering to escort me, meeting me at my apartment in Leme, taking the subway to Glória to his apartment and then walking just a few blocks to the "terreiro." It turned out to be eventful, perhaps one of a half – dozen such moments in Brazil, worth a section in itself in this narrative.

24

"Umbanda, Mediunidade" and Mike Gaherty

Sebastião explained just a bit about his connection to "Umbanda" as we walked from Glória and his apartment on Tuesday along the beach to the beginning of Flamengo, entering one of those narrow streets and stopping in front of an old, rather dingy building. The Batista family, like most in Brazil, were originally Catholic, but today are Baptists or Spiritists. He believes both in Kardecism and Umbanda, the first from Kardec's "Book of the Spirits" ["Livro dos Espíritos"]. Along with the Golden Rule, it is reduced to a belief in Reincarnation and communication with the spirits; the spirit of a deceased person can be "called" by the Medium, thus communicating with the believers who call for the spirit. Sebastião attends two different sessions: one Spiritism, the other Umbanda. He believes in both, and we are speaking here of a Brazilian intellectual and very rational person. He comments that both are both derived in part from Catholicism.

I had a thorough introduction to Kardecism years ago back in the Northeast in Campina Grande when friend Pedro Oliveira's Father, a famous medium, explained it all to me. Okay. So far, so good. But I had no experience with "Umbanda" and honestly had both a prejudice and I guess Catholic inspired fear of it.

First impressions of the "church, center or 'terreiro,' whatever you want to call it, were not positive. It is in a big old house in Flamengo. The floor was made of old wood and the walls had Indian bows and arrows (aluminum shine and color) and an old Indian headdress something like a Comanche headdress from the old cowboy movies I grew up on in Nebraska. There are images of Catholic saints, an altar with various images and images of Umbanda "saints:" including those of the "pretos velhos" ["old black men"] who supposedly were from the days of slavery.

The people attending seemed to be from the humble class. Upon entering, there was a short old man who collects pieces of paper, the prayers ["as preces"] which are requests for prayers during the session written on small slips of paper. The prayer slip is then assigned a number; it gives the person the right to "take a pass" ["tomar um passe"], in other words, to communicate with the spirit.

The session opens with the "smoke" or "purification" of those persons wishing to "receive" or communicate with the spirits or saints. Yours truly was keeping his eyes wide open during all this witnessing "that other world," and I was surprised to see Sebastião in the middle of it. He encouraged me to get a paper, write down a prayer request and be involved in the process. Out of insecurity and also the old Catholic practice to avoid such things, I chose to not participate, apologizing to my friend. At first that is.

Here is what unfolded:

1. The "smoking" or purifying chant: cleansing the area of negative spirits, that is of Exú (sometimes associated with the devil and notorious for interfering with rituals). This permitted the other spirits to enter. The "Médiuns" are the first to be cleansed.

2. Then purification by smoke of all the persons present, "preparing the atmosphere."

3. The song of invocation, in this case, to the spirits Oxóssi, Xangô, Iemanjá, Cosme and Damian. All these are also saints in traditional Candomblé from Bahia or Xangô from Recife, mainline Afro – Brazilian cults; the names were familiar to me. Then it got "weird" as other spirits were called: the "caboclos" or Indigenous Saints – Mirambá, "Caboclo Jurema," an indigenous saint, and the Star Guide, the spirit of the star that guided the Three Wise Men to the Christ child in the manger.

4. The principal saint of this "terreiro" is Caboclo Mirambá.

5. Each Medium (the person who has the gift/ power to communicate with the saints) approaches the altar, bends, and touches it gently with his forehead, a sign of respect and confirmation of his faith. Then the spirit takes possession of the Medium who is now making whispers and groaning sounds. Sometimes there is a stronger effect that shakes the person; this is called a "violent incorporation" when the spirit takes possession of the Medium.

6. There may be a snapping of fingers by the Medium (now possessed by the spirit) who ritually cleanses the "aura" of a person – participant with one of the prayer slips, thus cleansing any "negative emanations" that the person may have absorbed previously. Cigars are used and their smoke effects the "cleansing" of the "aura." One Medium cleanses the other.

7. At this point the "public" is allowed to enter the altar area, each person assigned a number (according to the prayer slip filled out earlier in the meeting.)

It was then that Sebastião motioned to me from the altar, that Brazilian gesture always funny to me but not then – the right-hand palm down and moving the four fingers bent perpendicularly backward and forward – it means "come here." I shook my head no, he repeated the motion, smiled and I could read his lips: "It's all right. No reason to be afraid." For whatever reason, there seemed no time to think, to refuse my friend whom I trusted totally, so I did it. As I walked up the two steps to the altar level, one of the Mediuns handed me a slip of paper and said, "No need to write the prayer; the Spirit will know."

One of the two "Médiuns" drew close to me, gave a greeting in a language I did not know, lightly embraced me, then began snapping his fingers (cleansing me, Sebastião later explained). Then the Mediun, already possessed by the spirit, asked a "god" or "saint" to cure me or fulfill my prayer. I gasped, "I have none; the paper is blank." It was at that moment something happened I cannot yet now explain: I felt weak, my legs seemed to give out beneath me, and I crumpled to the floor of the altar, but feeling totally calm with no fear and, yes, a whole feeling moving through my head and body, of peace, of light, or perhaps enlightenment. Sebastião and another man were holding me upright, that is, sitting upright, both with huge smiles on their faces. After what seemed an eternity (but Sebastião said it was only two or three minutes) I "came to," or felt like I was back to within myself, with an amazing overall feeling of peace. They guided me back to my chair with the other members of the public nearby, said, "Just rest, do not fight this moment; enjoy it."

The session ended with a chant, and all came to me, patted me on the shoulder or took my hand and smiled, saying "Bem Vindo. Paz" ["Welcome. Peace"].

It was still early evening and Sebastião suggested we walk to a nearby small café he knew well, eat something, and have a drink. He chose coffee, I chose icy Brahma. That was when he explained it all.

"Miguel, I would not have called you except I was sure what was going to happen and did in fact happen. There was no doubt in my mind; I know your thinking, your good intentions and good will, and that you are a genuine good person. That was all I needed to know. Please, please, pardon me if I made a mistake. But you should know this: there is no doubt now. You my friend have what we call "Mediunidade," a rare gift not granted to everyone. I for example have it in a very limited way. I and my colleagues are sure you were visited tonight by the spirit Oxalá himself. There can be no greater honor; he is the light of God the Creator himself. And Miguel, the Médiun has no control over which spirit adopts him. You have been what you call in Catholicism, "blessed.""

"Miguel, I am a long-time student of religion, of my native Catholicism and now Kardecism and the principles of Umbanda. This experience in our parlance and understanding is akin to what Catholics call Mysticism, similar but not the same. The famous mystics like Santa Teresa de Jesus, San Juan de la Cruz and others labored long and hard to work toward some moment of experiencing or being in union with God himself in this life. (He laughed.) We believe it is not that difficult, but the believer may have to make do with a lesser god, or saint, that is. What you do with this is your choice; you never have to attend another session, or you can come regularly. We will treat you the same. I do believe that from now on you can feel justified in being under the protection of Oxalá. You Catholics sometimes mistake this for what you call your "guardian angel." Perhaps. Perhaps. We believe it is God himself."

"Sebastião, I'm not sure where I stand on all this. There have been moments in my life where I have felt and been blessed, I am sure of that. And I have felt extraordinarily protected at several moments in life. I have never, on the other hand, felt the peace, the mental and physical peace, that I felt those few moments a while ago. Some Catholics talk about being "slain in the spirit." I think that is what happened. I am grateful for that and grateful to you. Do not fear for our friendship. You do understand that it will take some time to "digest" all this. I think I have had all I can take in for one moment of time. Can we perhaps discuss it again in a few days?"

Sebastião smiled, said, "Sure, in fact I will never bring it up. But I will know, and I will remember. I'm hoping some of your 'aura' can rub off on me! Just in case, Friday is "Table Day" ["Dia de Mesa"] at this 'terreiro,' a night of Kardec Spiritism; Tuesday, like today, is a 'pass day' ['Dia de Passe'] or Caboclo Spiritism. Friday is night of the 'Old Black Spirits' ["Pretos Velhos"]. You are welcome to join me any of those nights."

"I've had enough for now. Let's let it rest and I'll let you know."

"Miguel, there is one more thing I have not mentioned, and I think we should talk about it. It has to do with your writing, I mean your dissertation, and now all these books in Brazil including 'Letters.' Only one way to put it: Miguel, does it seem to come easy, do the words sometimes just come without great effort, study or thinking?"

I laughed. "There are times when the words flow easily and I'm not sure why. I always compare it to the Maya Lady I met in Chiapas who said the weaving patterns for her "huipiles" 'came to me as in a dream.' Many professional writers, novelists and such, say the same, but they also complain of 'writer's block.'" Mysterious stuff.

"Miguel, we believe in something called psychographic writing. The medium receives messages, text, even books, from spirits. There is one fellow in Brazil up in Minas Gerais who has 'written' literally hundreds of such books, 'dictated' by a deceased medium to him."

"I'm afraid that's a bit too murky for me, Sebastião. Not the same for sure. I appreciate your concern and interests. Let's leave it at that."

"I'm not trying to conjure up things or stir up trouble. Agreed. I do believe you had a spirit visit tonight. Lucky you."

We walked back to Glória and I got the subway back home, still good friends, and me the Brazil scholar with one more notch in the "folkloric six – gun."

25

LUNCH WITH CRISTINA MARIA

It may seem like I'm checking things off a list, and it is a little like that. This visit to Brazil would be incomplete without our conversation. That next morning, a Wednesday, I called the number Cristina Maria had slipped into my hand at the Ferreiras a few days ago, evidently a private phone at work. She seemed pleased by the call and said, "No sense wasting time, how about lunch today. I'll meet you at the Churrascaria in Copacabana at 1 p.m. All business, Mike, and no surprises. Topa?"

"Great, I'll see you at one o'clock."

When I walked in, she was seated at one of the tables out in the patio, motioned for me to come over and sit down. I did as she asked. We got the "light" lunch, not the whole shebang, but plenty filling with our choice of "picanha, maminha de alcatre" the sides of coconut flavored rolls, and the salad bar. I ordered one of the icy "Xingu" dark beers and she had a glass of white wine. She began what turned out to be an emotional conversation for the two of us.

"Mike, I just wanted some private time with you, first to reminisce a bit and then a family note." Over three beers for me and later their terrific coffee after the meal we did just that. In effect it was down memory lane, first, meeting her on the beach at Ipanema during my first year in Brazil, the sometimes "hot" dates in the Castelinho and listening to Chico Buarque on the national Song Festival Shows on TV. I thanked her again for that, "It opened up a whole new phase of my appreciation and love of Brazil." We talked of the "Michael Patriot – Cristina Maria Patriot" conversation two years later when she revealed her bad student exchange experience in Alabama and then swearing never to come to the U.S. again. It squelched any amorous plans for the two of us, me not willing or able to commit to life in Brazil either, not even dreaming of how I would make a living or adapt. Then we both laughed and remembered the Motel a year later and the lessons she taught me of loving a Carioca woman. Then she recalled my "comforting" her during bad times a year after that and both of us reliving the concerts with Chico and the tragic ending with the Vlado Merzog death and my eventually being asked to leave Brazil. Then the long hiatus, my absence from Brazil, the International Adventurer trips and relationship with Amy, once again gone awry. And now, both of us happily married with good careers, husband and wife, and children. Have I left anything out?

"It's been quite a ride Cristina Maria; let's call if 'Memories of our Youth,' not exactly a unique expression I suppose, but always a part of all these years. Like you said a few days ago, perhaps it was 'scripted' by someone watching over us. Any regrets?"

She thought for a moment and said, "I wish it could have been otherwise, and don't think I haven't thought about it off and on during all this time. But no, no regrets. It all turned out as it should have. She touched my hand, leaned over, and we kissed on the cheek.

"Mike, there is one final thought. I believe Mom and especially Dad always thought I had let you get away, Dad remembering he would have made a place for you in the firm. Both remembering a good young man from the United States with not much else ever good to say about that place. That's my point now. Dad is really failing, I'm just happy he will see his old Brazil, or something like it, come to pass soon. We all believe the twenty-year nightmare is about over. My request is simple: will you stop by soon, and I mean in the next few days or weeks and see him and Mom again? It's for me. Maybe closure for them as well. I doubt this could happen another year from now."

"I would not have it any other way; the feelings are indeed mutual, and maybe I can give you all a final moment of pleasure. This Saturday night Chico is doing a concert in the Maracanazinho and with a 'surprise' visit from 'Arretado.' We plan on a set of 'Mistakes of our Youth' and me with a chance to perform that one Brazilian song I learned and will try to stumble through, 'Manhã de Carnaval.' I understand it will be on TV Globo that night. It would be a great memory for your parents, and porra, you as well."

"Que surpresa! Count on us being tuned in. I'll tell Mom and Dad and maybe the whole family can watch. Just one promise: come and see us sometime afterwards so we can all reminisce and enjoy the moment."

"Agreed. I'll call early the following week."

When the check arrived, she pushed my hand away and said, "This one's on Brazil." My memory of her is driving away in the flashy sedan, waving goodbye through the window, and me beginning that ole' slow walk back to Leme and the apartment. Ah youth!

That night I called Molly again. Just moved to do so. We traded news and small talk; all is well at home and here. The big news was I told her about the concert coming up. Her take: get a tape of that Mike, for me. Promise?

26

REHEARSAL AND THE REAL THING

Chico called me on that Wednesday evening saying that a rehearsal is on tap for Thursday at the venue, and even though my part "is a surprise," better to practice. The band would pick me up on Princesa Isabel at 10:00 a.m. "Prepára-te a te divertir" ["Prepare to have some fun"].

The blue van with Chico, the lead and backup guitarist Toninho, singer Ginni, flautist Leão and percussionist Toca were all there. I was welcomed aboard and after some fast driving by their usual chauffer Manueli, in an hour we pulled up to the front of the Maracanazinho. First time for me; at first glance it appeared much like the basketball arena back in Lincoln, seating capacity I think at 14,000. I asked Chico what they expected for a turnout, he laughed and said, "Vamos ver – 10,000 fãs, 200 'macacos' dos DOPS" ["Let's see now, 10,000 fans and 200 'cops' from the DOPS"]. In this case the band would be performing on an elevated stage in the center of the basketball floor which rotated very slowly so everyone had a "front row seat." The equipment and sound team had arrived an hour earlier, and it was all set up with instruments in their stands alongside the mikes. A couple of very large coolers were replete with iced down beer, three or four bottles of Pitú Cachaça ("it's cheap, but it's the real thing from Pernambuco") and two members of the band pulled out their stash of "erva." Hmm.

I sat in a chair at the edge of the stage and just took it all in. The plan was for two full hours plus stage – calls, four sets – one with the 60s hits like "A Banda," a third for songs of the 70s including "Apesar de Você" and a fourth with 80s hits, including "As Tabelas." Between sets one and three the "surprise" would be Chico talking of nostalgia and a surprise return to "Mistakes of Our Youth" with our guest from 1971 - "Arretado!" Chico would do the old intro – talking about "old times" and how he got started in São Paulo with Rock n' Roll before "seeing the light" with Bossa Nova and then Samba.

We would do six rock songs, with Toninho now on a Strat and Toca on regular drum set. He handed me one of the guitars and said, "Bora" [Ok, now], and we did a medley of six tunes, the same ones as at Paecambú in São Paulo thirteen years ago. As we warmed up, the memories came back, the chords and the lyrics. We had to do it twice, but Chico was satisfied, "O,' ninguém realmente sabe inglês e muitas águas já rolaram. Se há um bocado de 'velha – guardas' tanto melhor." ["Oh, no one really knows English and there is a lot of water under the bridge. If there are a few old – timers present, so much the better"]. Then he got serious,

> "Arretado, você ainda topa para 'Manhã de Carnaval?' Toninho fará aquela famosa introdução de violão clássico, você acompanha no seu violão clássico, e canta os dois versos, menos o final; aí todos nós cantamos o mesmo e o final. Tá?"

> "Arretado, do you still want to do 'Manhã de Carnaval'? Toninho will do that famous introduction on a classic guitar, you accompany on your classic, sing two verses, not including the last, and there all of us will join in. Ok?"

I said yes and tried to do it but muffed the rhythm and the lyrics the first time. Toca came up with one of those "funny" cigarettes, said, 'Só duas inhalações e será melhor" ["Just two puffs and it will all get better"]. Everyone laughed, Chico said, "Um descanso enquanto Arretado melhora de atitude" ["Let's take a break while Arretado has an attitude adjustment"]. Even though I don't smoke the stuff, always nervous about it, this was different. And porra it worked; in just a few minutes I relaxed, and we did the song. Toca said, we'll do this out of sight behind the drums on Saturday and you'll be a hit! Pardon the pun!"

With everyone satisfied, we finished the session and made arrangements for Saturday. They would pick me up at seven, we would all go to a restaurant near the venue, have dinner (and lots of drinks), and arrive at the venue at 8:00 sharp, dress in the rooms set up for that under one of the 'arquibancadas'[stands]. Chico said, "They know you are a gringo, so dress like a gringo." "What does that mean?"

"Lousy, Arretado, lousy." I suggested casual slacks, loafers and a green turtleneck and an Irish cap." Gaherty, what else? Chico said, "Not too bad. It will do." And laughed.

I spent most of that Friday just trying to control my nerves. Another swim at Copacabana, but more careful this time and no accidents. I walked down to the "Braseiro" and had the old favorite meal, "arroz a grego, frango a passarinho, vinagrete, e uma cerveja fria." It just felt good to do the walking which included a couple of stops in bookstores and in one music store where I picked up a CD of Chico's latest. The rest of the day I went over the research materials gathered the past two or three weeks, organized them and finished, quite satisfied of the "haul." There was time to do a rather lengthy letter to the "Times" and then another call to Molly. I guess I was just trying to keep busy before tomorrow's big shindig but confess that I did another practice at home of "Manhã de Carnaval."

I slept in the next morning, practiced again, cleaned up and caught up on reading, this time with Luís Fernando Veríssimo'a latest, now a staple for my classes at Georgetown, especially on "culture day" when Verissimo's chronicles were perfect for the day to day living in Brazil and also day to day Portuguese.

The day dragged a bit, but it finally was time to get dressed and meet the van for what promised to be an amazing evening.

27

THE "SHOW"

I'll skip the dinner except to say it was at a Portuguese Themed Place – "bacalhau" [Portuguese codfish] and such – but they had old Brazilian standbys of "frango, bife, ou peixe" [grilled chicken, beef or fish] so it went well for me. Chico and the group sang "Tanto Mar" ["So Much Ocean"] for the customers and waiters followed by great applause and shouts of "Viva Portugal." There was lots of good Portuguese wine, in this case including my favorite of "vinho verde," that light wine with a fizz to it. And a subsequent buzz. We went over the sequence of the evening to come, Chico assuring me that all was well in hand. Okay.

The venue was just fifteen minutes from the restaurant; fans waiting along the curb and yelling greetings. Chico stopped to show me the kiosks in front of the main door with the names of all the Brazilian "craques" since 1950 when it all started in the Maracanã – Pelé, Garrincha and all the others. We walked to the dressing room beneath one of the 'arquibancadas,' dressed, and drank a lot of bottled water I might add. They informed us the crowd was rolling in, most singing old Chico favorites, and maybe more people than he had surmised – "Ótimo! Muita carestia estes dias – não faz mal" ["Great! There's a high cost of living these days. Pretty cool"]. I remained in the dressing room but could hear the roar of the crowd, Chico leading them on with cheers of "Viva Brasil," "Viva a Democracia." So far, so good.

They did a medley of the old 1960s songs, "A Banda" "Tem Mais Samba," and "Pedro Pedreiro." Then came "Juca" and "Meu Refrão," the crowd all on their feet and dancing. Chico took the mike and here's the rest.

"Amigos, we have an opportunity today in these good times to welcome back an old friend from 1971 and our series of concerts we tabbed 'Mistakes of Our Youth.' Most of you are too young to remember, ha ha, but 'Mistakes' was memorable and maybe a few of you can share it now – it's the Rock n' Roll I was playing with buddies in the 'botecos' of São Paulo as a teenager. I dreamed of being Elvis Presley, a good thing that did not happen. But a great new friend joined us in 1971, Miguel Gaherty, 'O Arretado' a colleague of research and 'farra,' both of us reliving 'Pedro Pedreiro' and "Asa Branca,' the 'Literatura de Cordel' and a campaign for jobs for the 'povo.' Bem Vindo ao Arretado!"

I walked out on the stage, acknowledged enthusiastic applause, picked up one of the electric guitars, Chico nodded and away we went. We did "Blue Suede Shoes" and "Heartbreak Hotel" by Elvis, then "That'll Be the Day" by Buddy Holly, "All I have to do is Dream" of the Everly Brothers and finally "I saw her standing on the corner" by Little Richard. It was near bedlam in the crowd with all on their feet, dancing and many singing along. Chico announced a final tribute to the first Rock 'n Roller, Chuck Berry and we launched into an ersatz "Johhny B' Good."

Chico took the mike, the crowd quieted down, and he said, "O' gente, I am fulfilling a promise to Arretado from 13 years ago when we were all on a roll before VIado Merzog. He knows 'gringos can't dance samba,' but he learned one of our best and his favorite which the band and I are going to help him sing, it's 'Manhã de Carnaval.' Vai, Miguel:

I sat down on a chair with a footstool, the nylon string guitar cradled across one leg classic style, said this song and "Black Orpheus" inspired my entire generation to come to know Brazil, and we all began the song:

> Manhã tão bonita manhã; De um dia feliz que chegou
> O sol no céu surgiu; Em cada cor brilhou
> Voltou o sonho então ao coração …
>
> Depois deste dia feliz; Não sei se outro dia haverá
> E nossa manhã, tão belo final; Manhã de carnaval.
> Canta o meu coração, alegria voltou; tão feliz amanhã deste amor
> (No translation – it can't be done!)

Then an amazing thing happened; the entire audience joined in and we all did it again. Loud applause and everyone standing on their feet. Chico looked over at me, nodded and twirled his right hand around with index finger outstretched. I said to the audience, "There's one more I learned on a sidewalk serenata in Olinda in 1966; let's all sing:

> Olé mulher rendeira; Olé mulher rendá
> Lampião desceu da serra; Desceu de Cajazeira. Bis.
>
> Olé mulher rendeira, Olé mulher rendá
> Que me ensine fazer renda; que te ensino namorar. Lampião, bis.

Leão on the flute and Toninho on guitar joined in and it was standing and applause again. Chico said, "In honor of and remembering o Arretado, o 'cordel' e nossa herança nordestina, aqui vai 'Asa Branca;' todos, cantemos! ["In honor of and remembering Arretado, 'cordel,' and our northeastern heritage, here goes 'Asa Branca.' Let's all sing!"]. Chico played guitar and Leão switched from flute to sound box. Luís Gonzaga would have been proud.

I walked off the stage with applause in my ears. A dream fulfilled.

The band and Chico went on to do those two final sets, songs from the 70s like "Construção" and songs from the 80s like "As Tabelas" and walked off the stage after curtain calls at 11:00 p.m. Chico was ecstatic,

> "Pessoal, sucesso! E ainda na TV Globo! As vendas e convites vão chover! Bora! Vamos empacotar tudo e ir à casa. Farra esta noite!"
>
> "Folks, a success! And even on TV Globo! Sales and invitations for concerts are sure to rain down! Let's pack up and go home to the house. Partying tonight!"].

An understatement! The band plus many of Chico's friends gathered at the house and the party *began* at midnight! Everyone replayed the events of the evening; most folks amazed the venue was full to capacity. And a congenial crowd, no problems, and no need for the DOPS to mess with us. I was congratulated on my part, most able to ignore the small mistakes brought on by nervousness. Toca said, "Mais toques de erva iam resolver isso!" ["A few more 'hits' of the 'erva' would take care of that!"]. And laughed. I thanked them all publicly, adding the praise for the northeastern songs and such. "Um sonho cumprido! Um momento inesquecível na minha vida" ["My dreams fulfilled! An unforgettable moment in my life!"]. The band discussed which songs seemed to have the most impact, a clue to future performances perhaps. Surprisingly enough, it all was pretty much as expected from the 60s to the 80s, from carnival and samba to social protest, but "As Tabelas" perhaps with most applause, maybe reflecting most recent times.

There were a couple of unexpected phone calls, the first to me from, well, Sônia, as promised. She was gushing and said we *must* get together to celebrate the moment. I said I would call in just a day or two, but was in no shape to make plans now, and guess what? She agreed.

The other call was as we say at home "from out of left field" - an old "friend," General Goeldi from the former censorship office. He talked to Chico and said, "Just as a favor, could you and Michael come down to the downtown office Monday at 3 p.m. to discuss the latest success?" He congratulated all for a wonderful, peaceful show. Chico had a private moment with me and said, "Arretado, I'm not suspecting any trouble, but this is one of those 'command performances,' we can talk tomorrow."

I don't recall too much of the rest of the evening except that it was great fun. I slept in one of the guest rooms, didn't get up until 11 a.m. Sunday and we had lots of strong coffee and early eats before I begged off and took a taxi back to the apartment and did a very long nap.

28

A LITTLE NOTORIETY IS NOT ALL BAD

Chico and I were in the taxi to General Goeldi's office at 2:30 p.m. on Monday and sure to arrive on time for the appointment. In the car Chico reiterated that he expected absolutely no problems from the General and was wondering why this sudden request. We would soon know.

We were ushered into the office, bringing back memories of 1971 when I was "invited" to leave Brazil, supposedly "for my own safety." This time it was like night and day, much like the original conversation prior to that of 1971 when the General gushed over "Mistakes of Our Youth" and what good public relations it established between Brazil and the United States. He also waxed enthusiastic then about the series of four concerts to come: at the War Memorial in Rio, Paecambu in São Paulo, at Itaipu, and finally at João Pessoa, the beginning of the Transamazonic Highway. All that came to a thudding halt with the Merzog affair.

He took the floor, as it were.

"Chico e Miguel, vi tudo na TV Globo do concert ontem a noite no Maracanazinho. Fenomenal! Um grande sucesso! Tudo de paz, nada de encrencas. Assim gostamos, nós, representativos do Regime. O', Capitão Heitor Dias esteve aqui hoje de manhã dando detalhes sobre a segurança, etc. E tudo, jóia! Se me permite, Miguel, a novidade de 'Manhã de Carvaval' foi um estouro! Parabens. E Chico tudo revelou 'bom juízo' por parte de você."

"Chico and Michael, I saw everything on the TV Globo Concert last night in the Maracanizinho. Phenomenal! A huge success! All peaceful, no problems. That

115

is the way we like it, we the representatives of the Regime. Captain Heitor Dias was here this morning providing us with details on the security, etc. And everything, wonderful! If you permit me, Michael, that new song on your part, "Manhã de Carval" was an applause maker, congratulations. And Chico, it all revealed good judgement on your part."

Chico falou, "Obrigado General, e em que posso ou podemos servi-lhe?"

Chico spoke up, a little reticent I think, "Thank you General. And What can we do for you?"

"Chico and Miguel, we figure you owe us one; I mean the cancellation of the last scheduled concert in João Pessoa to celebrate the Transamazon Highway, vis a vis the regrettable Merzog affair. But that was thirteen years ago, a lot of water under the bridge, and things are definitely looking better for all of us now. My colleague General Figueiredo is committed to the indirect presidential election next January, and between you and me, things are looking good for Tancredo Neves. We've had our time, accomplished much if not all we planned, and Brazil seems to be ready to move on. I'm thinking a reprise of the War Memorial Concert with the same program as last night, including Miguel, the Northeastern anthem and "Manhã de Carnaval" as well as 'Mistakes of our Youth.' We would provide security and a healthy stipend, Chico, this latter beyond ticket sales. What do you think?"

Chico sat for a while, pensive, and then spoke up: "General, honestly, Marieta, I and the band could use the money. We are a roll after Saturday, and I think we could get a good crowd. But there is a proviso or two: we would have to repeat the appeal of job benefits for the poor, especially the 'nordestinos,' with the set we did Saturday, and there would have to be a Democracy theme highlighting the 'manifestações para Diretas Já' ['Demonstrations for Direct Elections Now'] and for Tancredo Neves. (Chico did not talk of specific songs. I could not believe he *now in 1984* seemed to be in a position to *negotiate* with the government. How times have changed!)

"I'll think about that and will discuss with my colleagues, but Chico, I think and highly suggest that you just say something like, 'There is something new in the air, happiness is here, carnival and good times again.' Reference to 'Diretas Já' or Tancredo is not on the table."

Chico was quiet again, pensive, and finally said, "General I think we can arrange that. But you do your part, security, no roughing up of the crowd, and allowing the free spirit and joy to happen, which I think they will. Indeed, I think there will be dancing in the streets and a Carnival atmosphere. But you know I cannot control the audience."

"Chico, absolutely nothing nasty about the regime. Can that be a proviso?"

I could see Chico's mind a'whirring, thinking; he smiled and said, "It's a deal. When? I suggest next Saturday night. Strike while the iron is hot!"

"That gives us only five days; we can move very rapidly with the security. And we can put out notices to TV Globo and 'O Globo' this afternoon. It will be tight, but okay. Remember, no surprises, no nastiness, good times are here again."

We all shook hands. The General did not know of my "cordel" findings the past few weeks, nothing written up yet; *that* indeed would be a bit touchy when it would come out in "Letters," but I think tempered by the good feelings now of 1984. He thanked us once again and dismissed us with a smile.

Chico was ecstatic in the taxi, "Arretado, I did it, 'Driblei os generais mais uma vez' [I fooled the Generals one more time]. Indeed, there will be no nastiness and good times will reign, but I've got one surprise for them, a terrific new song which fits perfectly. We will rehearse it Thursday, but you might imagine; it's called 'Vai Passar.' Stay tuned. We can rehearse at the house; all 'hush – hush,' I don't want anything new to get out. I'll call the publicity team today and get the ball rolling for Saturday. Ticket sales to the public. Globo's payment. So, what do you think, one more time?"

"Seems fine to me, I'm getting a bit used to this notoriety."

That was true once again as I walked up São Clemente from the subway stop to the Casa de Rui that afternoon. Several people stopped me on the street and even asked for autographs from "O Arretado," and then Orígenes, Sebastião and the girls at the "cordel" library making much of it all. I told them about the War Memorial Concert to come the next Saturday and assured I could get them tickets. That included Cláudia after we had a friendly chat in her office.

29

FOR OLD TIME'S SAKE

I had some time before Thursday and the rehearsal and there was something I wanted to do – go back to the Benedictine Monastery and hopefully hook up with confessor Fray Eugênio. I called early Tuesday morning and he remembered the conversation from 1971, and the confession I might add. He said, "Miguel, time has passed, I'm really feeling my age, new hearing aids, but I would love to have you. I snuck a look at the Maracanazinho Concert on TV. Why don't you come for lunch in the refectory with all of us, and then we can have a talk. Do you still believe in confession? I'll walk and talk you through it. God forgives all 'meu filho.'"

It happened that very day. The subway from Princesa Isabel all the way to the Presidente Vargas stop near Candelaria and the short walk to São Bento. I've written of it several times before – the plain façade but the magnificent baroque interior, the São Bento Colégio to the side, one of the most respected in Brazil with no less than Heitor Villa Lobos as one of the graduates. Dom Eugênio greeted me at the door, we talked a few moments seated in a pew in the quiet nave and then it was time for the Benedictine 'almoço.' Salad, beans and rice, fish in sauce, heavy homemade bread, and water to be sure to wash it all down. All was in silence with a young monk in the black robe with hood reading from scripture. I felt in a weird sense "back home." The stark whiteness of the dining room with only a crucifix in the front, the tall windows facing the port and bay seemed familiar. There were fewer monks, but all in those dark black habits.

Then we had our quiet time (before his nap), alone in a corner of the main church. He was all questions: What happened in all these years since 1971? I filled him in, details the reader already knows. In turn, there were my questions for him, news of the Benedictines and the monastery. He once again talked of his age, now in his late seventies, the hearing aids that "gave me new life," and slowing down, much more difficult to kneel during all the services; "They give us old fellows a dispensation, but it's still a pain in the posterior sitting on the hard benches for what seems hours on end."

"There are fewer monks, but the Colégio does well, and our benefactors keep the bills paid. So 'quais são as novas'? ['What's new?']. And what brings you here? You are not quite that young man I remember from those years, that bigger waistline and less hair on your head. (He laughed.)"

I talked of the good fortune of the expedition ship Adventurer and trips to Brazil, Mexico, Portugal and Spain, the serious writing now of three books in the "Letters from Brazil" series, but mainly my marriage to Molly and little Claire (showing the photos from home). Oh, I did mention the move from Nebraska to Georgetown, continued liaison with "The Times" and now reporting and researching again in Brazil.

"Não é de admirar, ["I'm not surprised,"] recalling all the dalliances of youth, and I am truly happy for your marriage and the blessing of Claire. Hopefully there will be more children. I'm not entirely happy you are with the Jesuits again; they are our rivals yet, you know, but the Jesuit Colégio here now is all new theology, Liberation Theology at that, and their 'preference for the poor.' They probably have suffered more from the Military regime than any of us, but what goes around comes around. The Base Communities are a resounding success and their connection to the MST ("Movimento dos Sem Terra") ["Movement of Those Without Land"] has not earned them many friends among conservative circles here and all-around Brazil. It's the same in Argentina and Chile, but Georgetown is renowned and is what it is, with that connection to the government in Washington, D.C."

"Dom Eugênio, I admit to admiring their liberal cause, but I also remember their history, their missions, schools, hospitals and saints. Perhaps this is just a phase of history, and the pendulum will swing back with emphasis on the Spiritual Exercises. I think I like the idea of priests in the 'favelas' and working directly with the poor. How do you Benedictines deal with all that?"

"Miguel, it is simple and has to do with our Constitution and mission; we are largely contemplatives and trust that God himself will handle what needs to be handled, but don't ignore our significant works of charity which emanate from all our churches and monasteries, and, nossa! We have not done badly in our own style of educating the young. Nossa again! Some of the 'colégios' are now coed, and the St. Scholasticas are still doing a good job with the young ladies."

I commented, "I had a wonderful conversation with a friar at the São Francisco Church in Bahia while on the Adventurer trip a few years ago. He basically said similar things, but very sadly lamented the few new vocations and wondered of the future. He said they pray a lot."

"I would say his priorities are in order. We all need to pray more these days with the turmoil, manifestations and I believe imminent changes to come here in Brazil. We Benedictines have been at this in Rio since the 16th century, so I think God will find a way to keep us going. I do not want this to be a Benedictine – Jesuit debate; we all have bigger fish to fry. So let's do that conversation and I'll give you absolution when we finish."

Confession is sacred and sealed, but I can say to the reader that I filled Dom Eugênio in on the past few weeks, all the temptations with those former friendly Brazilian women and their charms, and that I indeed have been faithful, at least thus far, to my wedding vows and Molly, all really a very different story from 1971. "A different time Dom Eugênio, a different time. But it has not been easy!"

"Miguel, try it for fifty years! (He laughed). Celibacy does get easier, thank God, in one's seventies. And Molly I'm sure is waiting for your arrival back home."

"To be sure, that will happen soon, but hey there's a concert with Chico and the band at the War Memorial this Saturday, and that should provide enough excitement for me."

"I'll sneak another look at that on the TV. Just be careful. Anything else of importance?"

"No, but I want to thank you once again; this has been a wonderful reunion, and I will never forget the kindness and hospitality, *and* the counsel. You should have a few more years here, and I am sure there are many men and women who have received your counsel and are grateful."

"That indeed is the case. You are absolved of thoughts and deeds. God bless. It's time for that nap before evening prayers."

We embraced and parted I may say with some emotion on both our parts. I thought to myself that this could be the last time, but maybe not.

30

MUSIC, GOOD TIMES, AND CHICO'S SURPRISE

The rehearsal at the house was fun, a bit raucous and the songs went well, albeit with some stutter steps along the way. We are to meet at the house, take the van to the War Memorial in late afternoon, set up, and the concert will take place at 8:00 p.m. Chico informed us the publicity and ticket sales are going well, and that a general admission ticket at a reduced price will be available for those who ask for it, but seated on the periphery. The word is out, and he expects a big crowd on the spur of the moment. General Goeldi had called and said maximum security would be in place as planned and promised.

I can say I had time to telephone the Ferreiras and "the girls," all either promising to be there or watch on Globo.

It's here, the big day. And here's what happened.

Déjà vu all over again; a huge crowd all around the War Memorial grounds and the Aterro park to the side. Stage is set, oh, and Heitor Dias in his uniform best came up, smiling, saying, "Tudo em ordem. Manda brasa, chefe!" ["Everything is all set. Go get 'em, chief!]"

Okay. Set 1: "Mistakes of Our Youth," all the old, and I mean old, Rock n' Roll. The crowd singing along. How do they know those lyrics? Old farts, I guess.

Intervalo: Chico reintroduces "O Arretado" repeating the genesis: singing Rock n' Roll after many beers and "doses de cachaça" ["shots of cachaça"] at his house, the "idéia relâmpago" ["brainstorm"] for the LP and the concert of "Mistakes of Our Youth," the connection to "Cordel" and "Pedro Pedreiro," the planned four concerts until Vlado Merzog, and now 13 years later, the reprise! I very nervously managed to get through "Manhã de Carnaval" with the band's help. Amazing response from the crowd who sang along, and then all of us doing "Asa Branca." Delirious applause. Go figure.

Then the sets followed, highlights of the 60s, 70s and now 80s. Then the bombshell surprise: "Vai Passar" ["All This Shall Pass"]. It was Carnival all over again, all standing and dancing, and then cheering. Here is a selection from the lyrics so the reader can understand both the gravity of the situation (the possible end of dictatorship on the horizon) and the immense joy of the crowd, most who had participated in the "Diretas Já" manifestations.

> Vai passar, nessa avenida um samba popular
> Cada paralelepípedo da velha cidade essa noite vai se arrepiar, (ao lembrar)
> Que aqui passaram sambas imortais, que aqui sangraram nossos pés
> Que aqui sambaram nossos ancestrais.
>
> It is going to pass by, a popular samba on the avenue
> Each cobblestone of the old city is going to shiver (upon remembering)
> That immortal sambas passed by here, on our bloody feet
> That here our ancestors danced the samba.

The gist of it all (my paraphrasing) continued as the crowd was on its feet dancing: In another time, an unhappy page of our history, a faded passage in the memory of our young generation that was dozing, our entire country was so distracted, not perceiving that we all were swept up in gloomy transactions. Their children wandered blindly through the continent, carrying stones on their backs like "penitents" raising strange cathedrals. And one day, finally, they had a right to a fleeting happiness, a breathtaking epidemic that is called Carnival. Oh! Carnival again! Applause for the "wing" [Carnival samba parade dancing group] of starving barons, the block of the black Napoleons, and the pigmies on the boulevard. My god, come and look, come see from up close an entire city singing, the evolution of freedom [singing and dancing] until the rising dawn. Oh, what a good life, cheers, Oh what a good life, cheers! The flag of the general sanatorium is going to end!

It was the joy of "A Banda" of 1966 returned, but after twenty years, and Chico at his best in the contagious carnival rhythms and lyrics that had the entire country dancing! Only someone familiar with the Samba School Parades would get it, and the entire audience was familiar, Chico "nailing" the essence of the largely black participants in the Carnival parade. There was a delirious happiness in the dancing that night. Chico indeed had "driblado" the regime for the last and most important time. His allusions to the twenty years of darkness and efforts to "sanitize" the nation were there but were not there, depending on your point of view. No one, and I mean no one, could deny the promise of a rosier future to come!

The band had to repeat the song four times, four times! This was before Chico thanked the crowd and said goodnight for all of us.

No one wanted to go home, no one. There was a huge milling about afterwards, and on the way back to the van and what would surely be a raucous all – nighter at Chico's, Heitor Dias cornered me, saying he would pick me up tomorrow for a long session at the pé sujo. Command performance! But he was smiling.

I won't go into all that happened at that party at Chico's, suffice to say I was escorted into one of the guest rooms at 4:00 a.m. and fell asleep immediately. Well-wishers, family friends, and "penetras" [gate crashers], the joy of the moment continued. Chico was mobbed but in one quiet moment had a few words for me:

"O' Arretado. Que bom que você pudesse presenciar este momento, e contribuir. Obrigado. Como Orféu no filme, simplesmente, 'obrigado.' Falaremos mais quando tudo se calmar."

"Oh, Arretado. How great that you could be here for this moment and contribute. Thank you. Like Orpheus in the movie, simply, thank you. We will talk more when everything calms down."

31

THE RECKONING

I'll admit to being nervous about the meeting with Heitor, but my nerves were soon calmed. After a quick call informing me of the time, his black car with driver and him in the back showed up promptly at 5 p.m. that next day. I did not mind and had needed most of the day to recuperate from all the "farra" at Chico's. I opened the car door, jumped in and a smiling Heitor greeted me saying, "Arretado, this time I'm paying! Consider it a reward for that performance at the concert. We'll talk at the 'ponto' ['hangout']."

I never have mentioned the name of that "boteco" two blocks back from Avenida Atlântica in Copacabana. It's called "O Escritório," a bit corny but apropos for all the men who tell their wives they were working late at the office. Heitor was a "regular" and we were greeted by his favorite waiter Jair who had saved a corner table a little more protected from the traffic and street noise if that is possible in Copacabana. "Seu Capitão, you are keeping quite the company these days, I recognize 'Arretado' from the concert yesterday. I hope you had a good seat. The usual?" That meant a 'caipirinha' for Heitor and I asked for a Brahma. And the snacks arrived, peanuts and potato chips.

"Pois, Miguel, how's your head? How many 'melhoral' ['aspirin'] did it take to get over the 'ressaca'['hangover']? (He heehawed.) The crowd loved it, and no one got out of hand or smartassed, amazingly enough. You know our history with Chico's crowd. Overall, I thought it was great. You know I'm not a fan of the 'nordestinos' but I am trying to appreciate your "Cordel" research and their music; I have to admit 'Asa Branca' even brings a tear to these weary old eyes. But, 'rapaz' that solo of yours blew me away. My generation loved the Bossa Nova and Luís Bonfá, Vinicius de Morais, and 'Black Orpheus,' not because we are in love with the 'favelados,' but that movie had so much of what we loved in old Rio that it became a favorite even for the military. I was a young recruit then, just starting to work my way up the ladder."

"Heitor, exactly what did you love in old Rio in the film?"

"Mainly that Chick that Orféu fell in love with, and how they captured the spirit of Carnival – all the people dancing on the ferry from Niterói, the dancing on the old streetcar, the Samba parade and geez, that incredible scene with the kids on Babylonia Hill at the end. You literature people don't give us cops enough credit, for instance was it not, what do you eggheads say, ironic? Ironic that the movie ended at dawn with your song and the actress who played the heroine, her real name was Dawn! Did you know that?"

And I've got one for you Mr. Film Critic, did *you* know the actress was not Brazilian?"

"Porra! Não pode ser." ["Damn! It can't be"].

"Não, senhor, she was American, and her full name is Marpessa Dawn. You at least got part of that right."

Heitor was deep in thought for a moment. "Nossa. Now that I think about it, she seemed to dance samba different from the other black girls." His face lit up. "Aha. That's it, 'gringos can't dance samba.'" He asked for another 'caipirinha.' "Anyway, Babilônia isn't that way today, or Roçinha or any of the others. Drugs, crime, prostitution, and too many wounded or killed police officers trying to keep the rest of the 'cariocas' safe from the gangs."

I bit my tongue, knowing that probably was not all the story; the "take" I had on it was not exactly his - that there were renegade "para – police" on the "take" shaking down the "favelado" businessmen, and "disappearing" undesirables. I'm not so sure about all that either, but it is what is talked about by people you meet in town.

"Anyway, amigo, you nailed it, uh, that is with the help of Chico and the band. Your Portuguese and accent are good, but there is still a little bit of something of the gringo in it. That didn't matter, however. I have worked security at concerts for 20 years and have never but never seen a crowd so "in to" the music, and never with the spontaneous dancing and carnival atmosphere. I guess that's what Chico had in mind with that new song. 'Vai passar.' The samba parade I mean. Nossa, it's like twenty years ago when we were all watching "A Banda" pass by. The only thing I didn't get was the "penitentes" carrying stones and building cathedrals. Maybe he's talking about the black laborers who built our Metropolitan Cathedral, hey, that would fit. Like those blacks dressed up like Napoleon or rich Barons. You know everyone believes that Carnival is three days of happiness, and you can be whatever you want to be – Napoleon, a Portuguese Diamond Baron, merda, que sei eu? ["What do I know?"] Hey, I was bouncing up and down to the tune as well; you can't help it."

I did not, believe me, share my complete views on the lyrics. No point going there. Heitor then changed the subject, "Miguel I want the truth. How many chicks did you lay at the party afterwards? There were a whole bunch of them salivating over you from near the stage. Jesus, José e Maria, that was your chance."

"You will never know my friend. That is confidential. Let's say I did not do anything Molly would have disapproved of."

"O', that ole' story. I've seen you in action down at Maria Aparecida's place, and I remember that motel 'gig' with the Ferreira chick and the Othon party with Sônia Rodrigues. You can't fool me."

I changed the subject wanting to talk of the evolving political situation and thought now's the time. Maybe it was the 'caipirinhas' but Heitor drew expansive and surprised me a bit with his analysis.

"Miguel, you know how I think, you know my history and my job. I'm hurt that most Brazilians, at least half of them, never did recognize what we, the military and law enforcement, did for Brazil these last twenty years. I've lost several colleagues at work, some of them close friends, to leftist violence. The Brazilians think they had it rough. They have no idea what 'rough' means when you live in Cuba or Russia for that matter. Sure, we made some mistakes, but we did great things too. Enough of that. But, amigo, that had a small, unexpected benefit, me being assigned to keep an eye on you back in 1969, all our ups and downs, and our friendship today. I'll drink to that."

Another round, and we both are getting a bit woozy and maudlin.

I gave Heitor my best imitation of a man-to-man Brazilian embrace and said, "Você acertou. Eu te conto como um dos grandes amigos na minha vida. Como Orféu diz no filme, 'Obrigado.' ["You got it right. I want to tell you now; you are one of the best friends I have. Like Orpheus said in the movie, 'Thank you.' Time to get me home to bed."

That is when it happened. We were getting up from the table and heading down Prado Júnior to Avenida Atlântica where Heitor had arranged for the driver to pick us up. A van drove by, slowed down, and a bearded guy lowered the window and began firing. All I remember was someone yelling something like "Gringo filho da puta e hipócrita, traiu o nosso Brasil," ["You son of a bitch hypocritical 'gringo,' you are a traitor to our Brazil"], shots firing, Heitor jumping in front of me and taking the brunt of two shots to the stomach and my left arm hurting like hell and bleeding like a stuck pig. Heitor was down on the pavement, moaning.

Jair was suddenly there with the staff car (I can only guess he heard the shots), siren going, and others coming as well. A military ambulance pulled up, Jair said, "To the Military Hospital, I'll lead the way." Sirens blaring, luckily the hospital was in nearby Urca, so in about ten to fifteen minutes we were pulled into the Emergency Entrance, gurneys out and both of us carried inside. Heitor went right to emergency, me to some other place, god knows where, and a team of doctors were giving me a shot. I blacked out, but I guess they started removing the bullet and dressing the wound right away.

Heitor was another matter. It was all surgeons "on call," we would only find out thirty minutes later the gravity of the situation. Jair, a family friend as well, called Dorinha and said there would be an escort to the hospital. It turns out they live in one of those apartment buildings in Flamengo facing the beach, so that was not far away either. I was still fuzzy when Jair came in and said she was outside the emergency operating room, in the waiting room. The kids had been notified and were on their way.

Do you believe in miracles? I do now for sure. A surgeon came into my room after some time had passed, came to the bedside where I was resting and was told to drink lots of fluids and to not move around. "You are one lucky 'gringo,' Arretado." My left arm was bandaged from wrist to shoulder and hurt like hell, but an i.v. was dripping something pretty good into the other arm. I was awake but woozy. All I could say to the surgeon was, "He saved my life. It was me they were after."

The bespectacled Dr. gave a small smile and said, "Boas novas. Heitor is not going to die, that tough s.o.b. He took two bullets to the abdomen, one in the upper intestine, another just missing the abdominal aorta. If it hit that he would be dead. Both wounds have been addressed, the bullets removed, luckily it was not high caliber ordinance. There has been of course a lot of bleeding, part of the upper intestine cut out, and he is getting a big size dose of antibiotics as we speak. There will be a lengthy recovery. Dorinha is in the room now, but of course off to the side. But he did greet her, and she managed to give him a kiss on the forehead before we settled her down. A sedative was in order.

After that it was all a blur, me protesting, I don't know how much later, "I've got to see him, porra, to thank him." A nurse said, "Not yet, not yet, he will be there in morning and then we'll see. You are being kept for observation and perhaps for your own safety. Don't make waves senhor Gaherty, don't make waves."

They say a hospital is the worst place in the world if you want to get some rest, and this one was no different. I could hear all kinds of movement outside my room, muffled voices, and some angry words from someone, me just picking up words like, "We'll get those bastards soon enough."

An unexpected visitor was ushered into my room sometime later that night, no less than General Goeldi. Big brass has privileges, so if he wanted to visit, hospital staff did not get in his way. He pulled a chair up to the side of the bed, checked to see if I was awake. Semi-awake I would call it.

"Miguel, of all places and with all people, we did not expect *this* to happen. Heitor Dias has been in the line of fire countless times, but always on duty. As for you, I had planned a meeting with you and Chico early next week, to congratulate you, mostly, for the concert. Like Carnival and "Quarta feira de cinzas" [Ash Wednesday], I guess your revelry had to end. Believe me, this incident is top priority, and we will very shortly get to the bottom of it. I think they may release you tomorrow morning, but Officer Dias will be our guest here for a week or two. We are just all grateful it was not worse. I apologize ahead of time, but your privacy the next few days will be very limited; armed guards day and night, at least until we get to the bottom of all this. I'm sure you will understand."

He got up, smiled and said, "Lots of news for your "Letters" but I'm sure you will hold off on all that for now, right?"

The hospital kept me for one more day, but it was to say at the least eventful. Chico and Marieta were allowed a visit, and Sônia Rodrigues, I guess with her family "pistolão," ["pull"] was a surprise visitor. All wished me well, Chico's comments I leave for later. Sônia, well, she raved about the concert, actually both of them at Maraca and then the War Memorial. "Miguel, I don't know what you can do to top all that, but never mind. Rodrigues security is actually in contact with and helping the DOPS (we are long – time 'partners' as you know, unfortunately from 1971). They have leads and things are moving at top speed; I'll personally let you know when *we* know. And, it's on the house – no obligations, hein? Anyway, do you have a plan, I mean after they release you?"

"Sônia, I am grateful for your visit and, uh, your friendship. I'm so tired and sore now, there's nothing on the table. But you can call me, maybe more important, call the DOPS."

She came to the side of the bed, gave me a peck on the cheek and smiled. So be it 'Arretado querido!'"

32

RECOVERY AND TIME
WITH HEITOR

Later the next day, must have been mid – afternoon, they allowed me in to see Heitor. You could tell he was in pain and woozy from the sedatives they were pumping into him, but he recognized me, gave a small wave of his hand to "come over here," and smiled. "I took one for you my gringo friend, oops, I guess it was two. But I heard the bastard from the car. Cafajeste dos grandes [a real son of a bitch]. We are trained for what happened, but I must have been drunk. We only do that for political chefões [political 'big wheels']. I'm already thinking how you can pay me back."

I was in near tears, "Capitão, you did it for me, and you ole' velhaco, you saved my life. I think I know how I can pay you back, but let's save that for later. It won't hurt this much. I'll be in every day, and I'll help Dorinha. Get some rest. Back here tomorrow and I better not see any Marlboros."

"Não se preocupe. I'm hooked up to oxygen. Sometimes I'm stupid, but not that stupid." A faint smile and his eyes were closing, ready for more rest.

After that second day in the hospital, they released me. Rui and Marcela had seen the concert and the news on "Reporter Esso," and he requested from her full – time or at least part time, home nursing for me. She was not a nurse, but she knew enough to keep me comfortable, and may I say, first hot soup and good bread and then occasional meals. I was able to move around, painfully to be sure, but enough to get back to the hospital, have them check and redo the bandages, and most important, check in on Heitor. We had good but short conversations, and recovery had begun.

The big news, now day four after the shooting, was the news in "O Globo" and on TV and then a call from General Goeldi. Here first is the long news release in its entirety:

A Polícia Federal informou hoje a rápida resolução do ataque em sangue frio em contra o Capitão da Polícia Federal da Zona Sul, Heitor Dias, e o jovem professor – pesquisador (e não esquecendo, o 'parceiro' de Chico Banda e seu grupo nos concertos recentes no Maraca e o Monumento aos Soldados Caídos no Aterro) Michael Gaherty 'O Arretado.'

A segurança federal e da cidade do Rio traçaram os depoimentos de passeuntes no Prado Júnior, a descrição do van dos perpetradores covardes, e depoimentos dos feridos no Hospital Militar de Urca a uma residencia em um prédio de apartamentos em Niterói. Hoje de manhã os agentes do DOPS em pleno equipamento armado e roupas anti-bala de defesa, cercaram o prédio. Quando bateram na porta do/dos suspeitos, foram recebidos com uma chuva de balas de sub – metralhadora. Responderam com gas lacrimogêneo, granadas e balas de AK 47. O resultado: todos os suspeitos no apartamento foram estraçelados de balas e foram mortos na hora. Um polícia foi ferido e logo transferido ao Hospital Militar de Niterói.

O agente encarregado do grupo só disse o seguinte: "Uma pena que não houvesse chance de entrevistar os criminosos – terroristas. Nunca teremos uma explicação exata pelo ataque original no Prado Júnior. Só temos us palavras gritadas da janela do Van naquele dia: 'Gringo filho da puta, você traiu o Brasil.' Mas, não há dúvida de fatos fornecidos pelo próprio DOPS e a Agência Policial da Cia. Rodrigues que o grupo foi uma rama da velha ARB [Ação Revolucionária Brasileira] já ativa há anos em oposição armada ao regime do atual Presidente Figueiredo.

Estamos felizes a informar que o senhor Gaherty já foi liberado do Hospital e está em via de voltar ao normal. O Capitão Dias vai requerer umas semanas de descanso e recuperação, mas o prognóstico é favorável a uma cura completa.

Federal Police informed today of the attack in cold blood on the Captain of the Federal Police in the South Zone, Heitor Dias, and the young professor – researcher (and not forgetting, the 'partner' of Chico Buarque and his band in recent concerts in the Maracanazinho and the War Memorial) Michael Gaherty, o Arretado.

Security forces, both federal and those of the city of Rio traced statements from passerby witnesses, their descriptions of the van of the cowardly perpetrators of the crime, and statements by the victims in the Military Hospital of Urca, to a residence in an apartment building in Niterói. Early this morning agents from the DOPS in full armament and bullet proof vests surrounded the building. When they knocked on the apartment door of the suspects, they were received with a rain of submachinegun bullets. They responded with tear gas, hand grenades and bullets from their own AK 47s. The result: all the suspects were riddled with bullets and were killed on the scene. One of the security police was wounded and was transferred and is being treated at the Military Hospital in Niterói.

The agent in charge of the action said only, "A pity there was no chance to interview the criminals, that is, the terrorists. We will never have an exact explanation for the attack on Prado Júnior. We only have the words shouted from the van window that day: "You 'gringo' son of a bitch, you are a traitor to Brazil." [Author's query: is this "Yellow Journalism?"] But there is no doubt based on facts provided by the DOPS itself and the Security Agency of Rodrigues Limited, that the deceased criminals were a branch of the old A.R.B. (Ação Revolucionária Brasileira) active for years in armed opposition to the Regime, today commanded by General Figueiredo.

We are pleased to inform that Mr. Gaherty has now been released from the hospital and is returning to normal life. Captain Dias will require some weeks of rest and recuperation, but the medical prognosis is favorable for a complete healing.

General Goeldi had much more to say, but not over the telephone. He marked an interview with me and Heitor that p.m. in the hospital. Just the three of us were in the room, Heitor sitting up in bed with permission for just a short visit. The general first expressed satisfaction on my recovery in process and then cautionary optimism for Heitor who managed a laugh, weak to be sure, and smiled. Then a short statement by the General followed,

> *Capitão and Michael, the journal reporting the attack on you and your current status was for the most part correct this morning, but incomplete (out of necessary for security). I'm here to fill you in on a few small but important details, mainly what we believe was the cause. These were ARB people. By tracing personal documents in the apartment and scattered directives in their possession we learned that the three worked together, all in the van, a driver, the shooter on the right-hand driver's side, and his cohort with extra arms in the rear seat. Mike was the target; Heitor, sorry, you were in the wrong place at the wrong time but acted in a fully courageous manner that we expect of all our agents. So, no surprise to us, Captain.*
>
> *We are sure that it was an effort to embarrass the regime, after all we 'unofficially' were sponsoring the War Memorial Concert. More than that, it was a grudge going all the way back to 1969 when they tried to kidnap Mike at the Galeão Airport. You may recall that was handily thwarted by the SNI and the DOPS. There were no arrests at the time. This group, a small surviving splinter group of fanatics, was aware Mike of your current research and once again your link to the "New York Times" and the "INR." Your simple presence here now along with your reporting for them was just one more act of "U.S. Imperialism" and interference in Brazil. And for them "the last straw" was an "agent of imperialism" receiving such acclaim as a part, small to be sure, of Chico's recent successes. In sum, your success was their failure and by killing you they would in turn embarrass the regime."*

I was moved to respond, "General, what if I had not been involved with Chico and the research on his music and the concerts? Surely, I was putting him in danger just by my participation."

"True, indirectly, but the Left remembers Chico's criticism of the regime, until recently (I thought to myself - they still have not figured out 'Vai Passar'). You my friend were the embarrassment for them. Tio Sam's emissary, as it were, applauded by Brazilians. Now, back to you Heitor, the metaphoric bullet 'saiu pela culatra' ['backfired'] because you '*Coronel*,' made all Brazil proud of our security forces.

Heitor looked at the General, then me, and said, "Maybe it was all worth it. Colonel? Did I hear you correctly, sir?"

"Indeed, you did, effective today, and may I say, with significant benefits for you, Dorinha and the family. We do not forget our heroes."

There was silence in the room as Heitor pondered that news. Me too. The General took his leave, reiterating that this was a private conversation, wishing Heitor well "with the best of medical care" and adding a note for me:

"Michael, round the clock surveillance of you, your activities and whereabouts. We doubt what's left of ARB would have the, excuse me, balls, to try anything at this point. Just an insurance policy for you. By the way, what are your plans for the present and the next few days? Our choice would be for you to be on the New York flight tomorrow, but we cannot on the other hand deny your minor hero status in Rio these days."

"Honestly General I had not thought of it. My number one priority is to serve my benefactor hand and foot until he is on his feet. My research is concluded, music and concerts for sure. Just several loose ends to tie up, visits to research colleagues at the Casa de Rui, a parley with Chico and Marieta, seeing a few other friends in Rio, and a reunion with my student Flávio recently returned from Buenos Aires for what I hope are some quality visits.

"That sounds like a big order. Trust me, our men will be courteous but vigilant, and as far as possible 'in the shadows.' I'm sure we will be in touch. Thank both of you again."

He saluted Heitor, shook my hand and left the room. I just looked at Heitor and said, "Coronel, enough excitement for one day. I'll check back tomorrow." He smiled, patted my arm and said, "See if you can bring in one or two of those whiskey samples. We need to celebrate. I'll forgo the Marlboros for a bit. Uau, Dorinha may want to go shopping."

33

A Flurry of Activity

It was Chico and Marieta's first. I called and was told to come over to the house as soon as possible, and I did that next afternoon, me with the left arm still in a sling but gradually feeling better, no pain unless I touched it near the wound. I was welcomed with the usual embrace, but carefully on the other side. "How are you? We want the whole story."

I retold what I remembered of the attack, the hospital and the ensuing days including the contact with General Goeldi, Chico all ears. He and Marieta had of course seen the notice in "O Globo" and those details. He wanted to hear the rest, anything from General Goeldi. I was not at liberty, even with Chico, to repeat all that but did reaffirm that it was ARB, I was the target, and it probably was an attack on a U.S. "spy" and an effort to embarrass the regime.

Chico was pensive for a few moments and then "desembuchou" ["got it off his stomach"]:

"O' Miguel, eu me sinto culpado por isso, se não fosse pelos concertos, certamente não teriam atuado."

"Oh, Michael, I feel responsible for this. If it were not for the concerts, they certainly would not have taken action."

Eu aí respondi, "Chega amigo! Certo que meu pequeno papel exacerbou o interesse deles, mas, eu sempre andava como 'alvo' deles, e tarde, ou mais tarde, teriam feito um ataque. Azar foi que estivesse com Heitor Dias naquele pé sujo. Nunca te contei mas houve outra tentativa em 1969 quando estava saindo do Brasil.

Fiquei salvo, mas não posso falar de detalhes. Irônico! Agora devo a vida a um dos agentes principais do DOPS. Vou passar todo o tempo possível com ele e sua esposa Dorinha nos próximos dias."

I responded, "Enough already! It is true my small part probably exacerbated their interest, but I was always one of their targets. And sooner or later they would have made a move. The bad luck was that I was in that bar that day with Heitor Dias (or was it good luck?) I never told you that there was another attempt in 1969 when I was leaving Brazil. I was saved but I can't give you the details. It's ironic; I now owe one of the top agents of the DOPS my life. I'll be spending as much time as possible with him and wife Dorinha the next few days."

"O' gringo safado! Você no papel de agente da CIA! Brincando, mas graças a Deus está salvo. Como dizemos aqui, "e agora, José?"

"Oh, you shameless 'gringo!' You an agent of the CIA! Just joking but thank God you are safe. So what now?"

"I only want you to know, Chico you especially, that I feel no remorse for everything we have done together. The original research, the interviews, the articles published in 'Letters,' and especially all the partying, the music, and the concerts. My life turned into a real 'Rogue's Opera' ['Ópera do Malandro'] with real adventures, told, but not completely, in 'Letters.' And I owe in great part my promotion to Professor and the job at Georgetown to all this. Thank you, my friend."

Chico accepted the explanation, Marieta too, and the rest of that afternoon was a repeat, good food, drink, lots of laughter, the height of the time with them. They wanted to know my plans and I gave the short version – seeing other friends and a reunion with student Flávio (he had called telling me he was home from Buenos Aires and wanted a reunion as soon as possible). We had marked a day to celebrate later that week. There was an emotional goodbye, vows to get together again as soon as possible.

"Adeus."

During the next few days I began that sad cycle once again of saying goodbye to the wonderful Brazilians in Rio that have enriched my life. There was a visit to the Ferreiras, emotional because truly it might be the last time to see Jaime, and for that matter all of them. I simply did not know when I would ever return to Brazil. I think I saw Cristina Maria's eyes get a little moist, but all were so happy I was okay and said they would never forget our times together, from Chico in 1966 and now after the Concert. We wished each other well, talked of a "next time visit," and I said goodbye to Cristina Maria at the door. There was a close, close embrace with expected results, and she just smiled, a tear in her eye. Good memories, Miguel."

"Adeus."

The same day there was a visit to the Casa de Rui where I was welcomed once again, now as a minor celebrity in Rio, Orígenes, Sebastião and Cláudia all included. Most talk was of the concert, the attack, and now recovery, but Orígenes added a professional note: "We will be watching for the next version of 'Letters,' and I hope you are able to tell your entire story, but also what our poets of 'cordel' have reported. You will always have a chair at this table. In fact, I think we will make a plaque and it will just say, 'O Ponto do Arretado' ['Arretado's Place']. He laughed. Sebastião said to never forget our own "andanças" ["wanderings"] and hoped to see me again soon. Cláudia gave me a very close hug saying only, "Foi bom, não foi?" ["It *was* good, wasn't it?"].

"Adeus."

I called Sônia who was relieved at the recovery and surprisingly, I guess, just said, "Do you remember the promise?" I said I did, she said, "Good," and we hung up.

"Adeus."

There would be a final meeting with Heitor at the apartment in Flamengo, Dorinha whipping up a real 'carioca' feast. All the family was there, meaning the three kids, and of course, me. Heitor was now able to gingerly walk slowly and sit at the dining room table. He said, "Miguel, your favorites, all that junk food we used to eat at the 'pé sujo,' 'contra – file, fritas, vinagrete e muita cerveja gelada.'" We both laughed. There was a lot of reminiscing from those first encounters at the airport, the police sedan so many times in front of the Ferreiras, goodbyes at the airport, and now recent days. It was then I blurted out my idea for a thank you:

"Heitor, e Dorinha, after I get home and get settled in with Molly and Claire and the 'acadêmics' at Georgetown, number one priority will be to call in some markers with James Hansen at the Times and folks at the INR. How about that visit to D.C.? And I'll be your cicerone to see the sights, including a courtesy visit to FBI and CIA headquarters. You will be our VIP guest."

Heitor's eyes lit up, a huge smile crossed his face and then, dammit, some tears down his face,

"Miguel, that would be a dream come true. I hope it's not 'carioca' talk for 'Come on over to the house some time,' but coming from you, I believe it."

"No more to be said my friend. There is a lot to work out, but give me a month in D.C. You'll hear from me early fall."

That was our last face to face visit in Brazil. I would miss the customary visit and drinks at the airport. Now it turned out was time for my dream to come true.

34

"HOJE É SÁBADO" ONCE AGAIN

There was a joyful reunion with Flávio, once again on a Saturday. We met at his apartment where he told many stories of Buenos Aires and a probable move there to continue his editing work at least for the following year. More important was his reaction to recent events, "O' Professor, I thought I left you to that dusty library work at the Casa de Rui and figuring out 'a jeito' ['some way'] to deal with all your women friends. And, porra, look what you got yourself into? You always had great stories of Brazil in the classroom, but, ahem, I believe you outdid yourself this time!"

My arm was now out of the sling, just a day ago, sore, stiff, but mending well. I said, "Flávio, there are two or three things still to do. I've got travel reservations late tomorrow night with Varig to Miami and then on to D.C. Let's do that return to 'Guitarra de Prata.' I want to play that Del Vecchio if I can manage it and you have permission to 'one up me' with a Bach Fugue. Topa?"

That did not take that much convincing; we were back on the subway to the Rua da Carioca Stop and then the few blocks to the guitar shop. Pardon me, but everyone in the shop had seen the Concert and read of the shooting on Prado Júnior. We were waved immediately into Senhor Fornetta's tiny cubicle of an office. He was smoking of one those big Bahian stogies, laid it down carefully in the ash tray and slowly got up to greet us, a huge smile on his face.

"Bom Giorno, jovens artistas. I wondered if I would see you again or if that afternoon and promise a month ago were all talk. I should never have doubted you. Sit down, sit down, and tell an old man how you are doing. Miguel, I saw all the reporting on TV of the concert with Chico, that not – too – bad 'Manhã de Carnaval, and I only lament that your 'violão' ['guitar'] was just okay." He laughed long and hard. "Then just days ago came the reports of the shooting and the notice in "O Globo" you were allowed to go home. Thinking about it then, I could not believe that 'Arretado' and his great Italian friend Flávio had been here in my humble shop. Welcome back; this calls for a celebration." He pulled a bottle of Italian Orange Liqueur out of a desk drawer, found three small glasses which could not have been other than crystal from Venice, and poured generous dollops in each. "Salute. I am full of questions for both of you, Miguel we know more about, but how about you Flávio?"

Flávio regaled us then with tales from San Telmo in Buenos Aires and told of the good wine and Italian food and his frustrated efforts to learn 'lunfardo.' (I think I've already said he is fluent in English, Spanish, Portuguese *and* Italian.)

Senor Fornetta laughed, spoke up, "I've been right there and have seen more quality tango shows than you can imagine. Ah juventude! [Ah, youth!]! But I share your language difficulty. You know many Porteños can speak 'la vera lingua' when they want to. I recall Lunfardo as mainly a kind of 'ersatz' Italian, speaking street Spanish with Italian slang and accent. Que sei eu! [What do I know!] But, as we say, back to business, and I already know, you want to play the Del Vecchio." He motioned for an employee, jabbered something in very fast Portuguese, and within minutes it was on a side counter in the office.

I was transported once again to guitar heaven. I held the instrument and tried to play some of the old pieces. Turns out the shoulder and arm would not permit it. I handed it carefully to Flávio, smiled and said "O' carioca, dê – nos um show." Hearing Flávio's "dedilhar" [fast fretting and fingering] through Bach classics, and some Vivaldi and Scarlatti for good measure brought tears to my eyes.

I could not stand it any longer, "Senhor Fornetta, I want to buy this instrument and take it home to my other girl friend the Di Giorgio and see if they get along. Trouble is, I'm on limited cash for the trip, but I can cross my Irish heart and swear by all the saints including St. Brendan, that I will wire you the total cost in less than a week from home. All we have to do is agree on the price."

"Senhor Miguel 'Arretado,'as I told you some weeks ago, things have changed considerably since 1966 when you bought the Di Giorgio. This rare, fine instrument is now $5000 USD. I do not think you are ready for that; this 'garota carioca' ['carioca chick'] may be one of the best in town if not in all Brazil." He stopped for a moment, seemed deep in thought, and smiled, "I have an idea. You may not realize it, but you are a 'figura muito badalada' ['well known person'] now in Brazil, vis a vis that last concert with Chico, and I'm sorry, the unpleasant business of the attack, bullet wound and hospitalization. If you would allow me to use your name in advertising for our humble shop, and more so, as an owner of a Del Vecchio, I could offer it to you for $3000."

I did a mental calculation of our savings back home. Let's see, shoes and nice dresses for Claire, a night out now and again for Molly and me; a new car or a larger apartment in D.C. would have to wait. I could manage it. My young wife Molly would possibly understand. (I have not mentioned that I called her from the hospital using a DOPS line telling her of the shooting, but that I was just fine and would be home soon, knowing that the incident might appear as a footnote in the American press.)

"Negócio feito, [Done deal,] Senhor Fornetta! You have fulfilled a dream! A dream almost fourteen years old. Let's be sure to find one very sturdy case so I can get it home safely on Varig. I don't know if I told you but in 1966, I took that Di Giorgio home in a taxi to my host's house in Flamengo, cradled in my arms, and put it under a bed until I left for home. And then came the humungous battle I had with Pan Am to put it in the first-class coat closet for the ride home; I was seated way back in coach."

Senhor Fornetta smiled, shook my hand and refilled the glasses. "Salute! Miguel, you have made me very happy. This will all turn out well for both of us. And Flávio, 'amico,' you are always invited to my store to play any instrument you like, just with the condition I know ahead of time and can advertise the 'virtuoso' playing once again in 'Guitarra de Prata.'"

I can tell the reader now that it all came to pass, that is, getting Del Vecchio home, going to the bank and sending the $3000 by wire service. Perhaps someday I can play it in concert, even a tiny venue, one of my lifelong dreams, but surely it will not gather dust in D.C.

We all shook hands, abraços all around, albeit not on my left shoulder and promises to meet again. I told Flávio *I* would foot the bill for the taxi to my apartment, my good right arm cradling my new love beside me in the middle of the back seat.

"Now, velho ex-estudante, there is one last wish and commitment. I'm leaving late tomorrow at the Galeão, but we have an rendezvous on Babilônia Hill for the sunrise. Can you swing it and keep us safe?"

"Professor, I've lived here long enough that they know me up the hill, and if I just give the word, there are some 'capoeira' buddies who will keep an eye on us. Porra, I could do it myself, I know all the 'toques.' When shall we start the 'farra?'"

"That is a problem. I can't last all night long like you youngsters. How about an early dinner on Copa beach about 5:00 p.m., we drink 'uns e outros,' and some cafezinhos. I'll go home and pack, get a little sleep and we'll walk up the hill an hour before sunrise. Oh, you'll have to bring a guitar. Mine won't do. Ha ha."

"Professor, it couldn't be better. I'll contact the 'colegas' up in the 'favela,' and we will have a personal escort up the hill. It's not a paved sidewalk, but a good trail on gravel through the 'floresta.' Don't worry about a thing; I think your and perhaps my reputation precede us. You may have to sign some autographs. Bring a BIC. Ha ha."

I won't go into detail about that afternoon and early evening, mostly a repetition of our former reunions. Over "petiscos" of boiled shrimp and other goodies, and way too many Brahma choppes, we reminisced once again of the past at Georgetown, got caught up on San Telmo and my doings in Rio during Flávio's absence in Buenos Aires. Lots of old jokes, Flávio's imitations of all the language professors at Georgetown, including the "plain vanilla" Gaherty, much discussion of the Academy and the downward "spiral" it was taking in departments of Literature with the ever more esoteric "approaches" or "enfoques" to explain something that does not need explaining, that is, for the most part. My mantra in simpler days and mainly on the undergraduate level was read, read and enjoy, read the best. Literary Criticism is there *only* when you get in a jam. "Ulysses" a primary example, or maybe "Grande Sertão: Veredas." Flávio said, "It's all complex today. Your taste for Jorge Amado or Luís Fernando Veríssimo would be considered either puerile or just 'not real literature.'"

I could only think of the "big dog literary critic" back at Nebraska (Is their such a thing? Images flash by: "Good Will Hunting," "Big Dog Hunting," pheasants, ducks and cranes along the Platt. Sorry, the mind wanders. A lousy image.) who considered the "literatura de cordel" as "para – literature." Unfortunately, Aurélio Buarque de Hollanda's view in the big Dictionary was not better, maybe even worse. (Did I ever take that up with Chico?) Fortunately, it is all water under the bridge. Times have indeed changed, but it took a snooty professor from the Sorbonne to change the Brazilian peacock professors' minds. Ah, Vive la France! Ah, Français! Ah, gay Paree! Thank you, Mr. Snooty Professor.

35

THE SUN WILL COME UP

Flávio would have kept up the partying, but I had things to do. All the research materials to be packed, clothes, film, and Senhor Del Vecchio (masculine: "o violão" in Portuguese). I probably did not get to bed until 11:00 and sleep was fitful. An alarm went off at five, Flávio was there at six and the adventure began.

The street up to Chapéu Mangueira and over to old Babilônia Hill begins up the steep incline with his apartment building at its base. Three black guys, all about Flávio's age, met us outside his door, shook hands with me and called me "Arretado," One said, "I have to admit Chico is the best *white* imitation of the real thing." And they all laughed. We trudged up the steep narrow road for a while and then came into the edge of the "favela" where there was a mandatory stop at a 'botequim' with probably three large buckets filled with ice, beer and cachaça all cheerfully carried by those guys, all looking plenty strong from I guess the beach and capoeira. I picked up the tab, not outlandish compared to U.S. prices, but a necessity? "Você estará brincando?"

From then it was a narrow trail with thick vegetation on both sides until we reached the top: there it was! In the pre -dawn light in front and slightly below us the Morro da Babilônia, the beach of Urca and water down below, Pão de Açucar looming in the mist to the right, and beyond that the bay. Two words: "Orféu Negro." There was only about one – half hour to dawn and some serious drinking took place, Flávio joking with his cohorts who called him "O Professor." I spoke up, "Está na hora, Flávio."

He tuned the guitar, handed it to me, and with great difficulty I managed the simple chords and sang,

> Manhã tão bonita manhã; De um dia feliz que chegou
> O sol no céu surgiu; Em cada cor brilhou
> Voltou o sonho então ao coração ...
> Depois deste dia feliz; Não sei se outro dia haverá
> E nossa manhã, tão belo final; Manhã de carnaval.
> Canta o meu coração, alegria voltou; tão feliz amanhã deste amor."

And the sun rose once again over the morning mist.

I handed Flávio the guitar and he played a wonderfully enhanced guitar accompaniment, and we sang it again. There were no small children dancing, and you can't go home again, but the magic was still there.

"Porra, Flávio, o sonho voltou!"

I won't say we carefully picked our way down the hill; it was more like "slippin' and a' slidin" from some old Rock n' Roll piece. Uh oh, shouldn't have said that. Ignore it. We can't besmudge the moment.

We went to his place, finished off the beers, said a teary goodbye. Flávio said, "O' Professor, nem idéia como isto preencheu meu coração de alegria. Foi meu momento também." ["Oh, Professor, you have no idea how this filled my heart with happiness. It was my moment too."] There were embraces, vows of reuniting at the same time and same place and do it all over again. Such are the things you say, and maybe knowing deep down, "O dia de São Nunca." ["The Day of St. Never"]. No matter. No matter.

36

BREAKING THE RULES OF GOOD WRITING, ALL ANTI – CLIMACTIC

I slept all that morning and until early afternoon. The doorbell rang and it was Rui and Marcela, wondering what had happened to the renter. A good thing. I woozily woke up, showered, had a last "lanche" from Marcela, piled all my stuff into a radio – taxi (no taking chances huh?) and headed to the Galeão. I found out later there was no cause for concern; General Goeldi's friends were keeping a watch the whole way. I won't say there was little emotion on that ride repeating the route of the first time in Rio, but in reverse – through the tunnel, along the Aterro to downtown, Avenida Rio Branco, then Presidente Vargas and the road to the island and the airport. So many times, so many memories. Different this time.

Something else different – no Heitor Dias to give me last minute advice and a bear hug. One thing did repeat itself, from that time years before when I was coming down from Recife to leave the same night, but 24 hours late and Varig put me in business class to Chicago for my troubles. When I was checking in at the counter, the pretty Varig girl said, "Mr. Gaherty – Arretado, there's a mistake on your ticket. I have to talk to my supervisor."

"Oh crap, not again. I had the damned exit slip, crumpled in my billfold now for weeks, passport and visa in hand."

A smiling Varig supervisor, just as pretty, came in a few minutes, apologized, said she was sorry, but they would have to emit a new ticket. She smiled as the machine spit out a first – class ticket to Miami.

"Mr. Gaherty, our thanks for the wonderful moments you gave us on TV Globo with Chico, but also for all you have been through the last few days. We just happen to have two seats free in the front of the airplane, one for you and one for that handsome guitar case."

The reader wonders, is this just a "Be happy" fluffy ending to Gaherty's Brazilian Odyssey? You decide.

After my profuse thanks and a big hug to both Varig girls who gave me hugs and I daresay kisses in return, I had a full hour to wait before boarding. They offered me free drinks in the VIP suite which I graciously turned down. There could be no other ending than a sandwich and cold beers in that old lounge, somehow still preserved in the gelid, anti – septic Galeão, the one with all the tiles of the old propeller airplanes, bi – planes and WW II vintage fighters. This was where I had always chosen, when possible, the last hours in Brazil and where I had time to think, reminisce and write those diary notes. "Assim foi." ["So it went."]

EPILOGUE

There was a wonderful teary reunion at Dulles with wife Molly and beautiful toddler Claire in hand, the taxi ride home, dinner with champagne to accompany hours of telling tales, mine not as important as hers. And an intimate reunion after the wear and tear of it all, I mean Brazil, sent us both off to sleep.

Other later happenings:

Back to classes at Georgetown and Father Ricci's approval

A visit to New York and interview with James Hansen, happy to know I was safe and giving his approval for Letters IV

Heitor Dias and wife Dorinha come to D.C. The FBI and his dreams fulfilled

1985 Tancredo Neves is elected as the new president of Brazil but via indirect election. Shortly before inauguration day, he suffers a fatal sickness, several surgeries and dies days later in São Paulo. Vice President José Sarney takes over for the turbulent years ahead.

The "Literatura de Cordel" reports it all.

ABOUT THE AUTHOR

Mark Curran is a retired professor from Arizona State University where he worked from 1968 to 2011. He taught Spanish and Portuguese and their respective cultures. His research specialty was Brazil and its "popular literature in verse" or the "Literatura de Cordel," and he has published many articles in research reviews and now some seventeen books related to the "Cordel" in Brazil, the United States and Spain.

Other books done during retirement are of either an autobiographic nature – "The Farm" or "Coming of Age with the Jesuits" - or reflect classes taught at ASU on Luso-Brazilian Civilization, Latin American Civilization or Spanish Civilization. The latter are in the series "Stories I Told My Students:" books on Brazil, Colombia, Guatemala, Mexico, Portugal and Spain. "Letters from Brazil I, II, and III" is an experiment combining reporting and fiction. "A Professor Takes to the Sea I and II" is a chronicle of a retirement adventure with Lindblad Expeditions on their flagship the National Geographic Explorer. "Rural Odyssey – Living Can Be Dangerous" is "The Farm" largely made fiction. "A Rural Odyssey II – Abilene – Digging Deeper" and "Rural Odyssey III Dreams Fulfilled and Back to Abilene" are a continuation of "Rural Odyssey." "Around Brazil on the 'International Traveler' – A Fictional Panegyric" tells of an expedition in better and happier times in Brazil, but now in fiction. The author presents a continued expedition in fiction "Pre – Columbian Mexico – Plans, Pitfalls and Perils." Yet another is "Portugal and Spain on the 'International Adventurer.'" "The Collection" details Curran's primary and secondary works on Brazil's "Literature de Cordel" now housed at the Latin American Library of Tulane University. And now, the final in the series, "Letters from Brazil IV."

PUBLISHED BOOKS

A Literatura de Cordel. Brasil. 1973

Jorge Amado e a Literatura de Cordel. Brasil. 1981

A Presença de Rodolfo Coelho Cavalcante na Moderna Literatura de Cordel. Brasil. 1987

La Literatura de Cordel – Antología Bilingüe – Español y Portugués. España. 1990

Cuíca de Santo Amaro Poeta-Repórter da Bahia. Brasil. 1991

História do Brasil em Cordel. Brasil. 1998

Cuíca de Santo Amaro – Controvérsia no Cordel. Brasil. 2000

Brazil's Folk-Popular Poetry – "a Literatura de Cordel" – a Bilingual Anthology in English and Portuguese. USA. 2010

The Farm – Growing Up in Abilene, Kansas, in the 1940s and the 1950s. USA. 2010

Retrato do Brasil em Cordel. Brasil. 2011

Coming of Age with the Jesuits. USA. 2012

Peripécias de um Pesquisador "Gringo" no Brasil nos Anos 1960 ou A Cata de Cordel" USA. 2012

Adventures of a 'Gringo' Researcher in Brazil in the 1960s or In Search of Cordel. USA. 2012

A Trip to Colombia – Highlights of Its Spanish Colonial Heritage. USA. 2013

Travel, Research and Teaching in Guatemala and Mexico – In Quest of the Pre-Columbian Heritage
    Volume I – Guatemala. 2013
    Volume II – Mexico. USA. 2013

A Portrait of Brazil in the Twentieth Century – The Universe of the "Literatura de Cordel." USA. 2013

Fifty Years of Research on Brazil – A Photographic Journey. USA. 2013

Relembrando - A Velha Literatura de Cordel e a Voz dos Poetas. USA. 2014

Aconteceu no Brasil – Crônicas de um Pesquisador Norte Americano no Brasil II, USA. 2015

It Happened in Brazil – Chronicles of a North American Researcher in Brazil II. USA, 2015

Diário de um Pesquisador Norte-Americano no Brasil III. USA, 2016

Diary of a North American Researcher in Brazil III. USA, 2016

Letters from Brazil. A Cultural-Historical Narrative Made Fiction. USA 2017.

A Professor Takes to the Sea – Learning the Ropes on the National Geographic Explorer.
    Volume I, "Epic South America" 2013 USA, 2018.
    Volume II, 2014 and "Atlantic Odyssey 108" 2016, USA, 2018

Letters from Brazil II – Research, Romance and Dark Days Ahead. USA, 2019.

A Rural Odyssey – Living Can Be Dangerous. USA, 2019.

Letters from Brazil III – From Glad Times to Sad Times. USA, 2019.

A Rural Odyssey II – Abilene – Digging Deeper. USA, 2020

Around Brazil on the "International Traveler" – A Fictional Panegyric, USA, 2020

Pre – Columbian Mexico – Plans Pitfalls and Perils, USA 2020

Portugal and Spain on the 'International Adventurer,' USA, 2021

Rural Odyssey III – Dreams Fulfilled and Back to Abilene, USA, 2021

The Collection. USA, 2021

Letters from Brazil IV. A Time to Hope. USA, 2021

Professor Curran lives in Mesa, Arizona, and spends part of the year in Colorado. He is married to Keah Runshang Curran, and they have one daughter Kathleen who lives in Albuquerque, New Mexico, married to teacher Courtney Hinman in 2018. Her documentary film "Greening the Revolution" was presented most recently in the Sonoma Film Festival in California, this after other festivals in Milan, Italy and New York City. Katie was named best female director in the Oaxaca Film Festival in Mexico.

The author's e-mail address is: profmark@asu.edu
His website address is: www.currancordelconnection.com

Printed in the United States
by Baker & Taylor Publisher Services